CHRISTMASTIDE WITH HIS COUNTESS

ELLIE ST. CLAIR

CONTENTS

THE DUKE SHE WISHED FOR

QUEST OF HONOR

Facebook: Ellie St. Clair

Cover by AJF Designs

Do you love historical romance? Receive access to a free ebook, as well as exclusive content such as giveaways, contests, freebies and advance notice of pre-orders through my mailing list!

Sign up here!

Also By Ellie St. Clair

Standalone
Unmasking a Duke
Christmastide with His Countess
Seduced Under the Mistletoe Multi-Author Box Set
(featuring The Duke of Christmas)

Happily Ever After
The Duke She Wished For
Someday Her Duke Will Come
Once Upon a Duke's Dream
He's a Duke, But I Love Him
Loved by the Viscount
Because the Earl Loved Me

Searching Hearts
Quest of Honor
Clue of Affection

Hearts of Trust
Hope of Romance
Promise of Redemption

PROLOGUE

August, 1813

"Wilt thou have this man to be thy wedded husband, to live together after God's ordinance in the holy estate of Matrimony? Wilt thou obey him, and serve him, love, honor, and keep him in sickness and in health; and, forsaking all other, keep thee only unto him, so long as ye both shall live?"

An eerie silence came over the church as Scarlett stood there, breathing shallowly, heart pounding hard in her chest. She longed to toss her bouquet of herbs and pansies over the altar and turn on the heel of her soft pink kid slipper and run down the aisle — alone — just as fast as she possibly could.

She heard a cough behind her, a few muttered words, some whispers.

Out of the corner of her eye, she studied the stranger who stood at her elbow, now shifting back and forth from one foot to the other.

He was tall, much taller than her own average height. He

was attractive, to be sure, the structure of his face chiseled as though it had been sculpted by a master. His dark, nearly black locks circled his head in a symphony of curls. She wasn't sure what color his eyes were, for she had yet to actually look at them.

The first time they had met was moments ago, when her father had deposited her here, at the front of the quaint village church.

She ran all of her options through her mind once more and eventually came to the only possible conclusion, the one that had led her here this morning.

"I will."

When she finally said the words, they rang out with strength and clarity, for Scarlett never said anything she didn't truly mean. She would marry him. She had no choice, despite the stirrings deep inside her soul that cried out for freedom. But freedom, it seemed, was proving elusive — for the moment, at least.

After confirming it was her father giving her hand away — of course, for she was moving from being considered one man's property to another's — the minister continued, placing her right hand in her betrothed's.

Her skin tingled where they touched, despite the thin material of her glove between them. As he repeated the words given to him by the minister, Scarlett finally looked up at him. She hadn't meant to, but it was as though she had no choice. She locked eyes with him, and once she did, she wished she hadn't.

For his eyes were of a blue-green unlike any color she had ever seen before, except perhaps in a body of water on a dark day. And it seemed they almost ... twinkled? She blinked, trying to break the spell they had seemingly cast over her, but it was as though she was losing herself in their depths, drowning despite her best efforts to break through to the surface.

His voice was a silky smooth baritone, though she hardly heard a word that he said.

Suddenly there was silence again, and his lips turned up as he looked down at her. Was he nearly laughing? She stared back at him incredulously — what on earth was funny about this? Until she realized it was her turn to speak. Again.

"Can you repeat that?" she whispered to the minister, and he looked perturbed but did as she asked.

"I, Scarlett, take thee...." Oh, blast. What was his name again? Had the minister told her? She looked from him to her betrothed once more, and now his lips really did stretch out into a grin.

"Hunter," he supplied in a murmur, leaning into her, flustering her even more.

"Yes, I know, Hunter," she said. *Get a hold of yourself, Scarlett. You don't even want this wedding.* "I, Scarlett, take thee, Hunter, to be my wedded husband, to have and to hold from this day forward, for better for worse, for richer for poorer, in sickness and in health, to love, cherish, and to obey, till death us do part, according to God's holy ordinance; and thereto I give thee my troth."

The blessings and prayers went by quickly, and suddenly, nearly before she even realized it, the wedding was over, and her new husband — *husband* — was walking her down the aisle and out of the church.

Good Lord. What had she done?

HUNTER EYED the woman standing beside him. She was an

attractive woman, that was to be sure. Her hair was a deep chestnut with a touch of color that reminded him of cinnamon flowing through it. A smattering of freckles dusted her flawless skin, which was somewhat darker than the porcelain of other young women with whom he was familiar. It was as though she spent time outdoors. Not that he would know. He knew nothing about her. He had barely known her name until today, for goodness sake, and she had certainly forgotten his.

Their marriage had been an arrangement between their parents. His father was a powerful marquess, hers an earl. There had been a planned meeting between the two of them, of course, but her parents had told him she was ill. As he spent nearly all of his time in London and she had always been in the country, another suitable time never arose. Finally, the wedding day was planned, arrived, and here they were.

He hadn't even been sure she would be in attendance at the ceremony, despite her father's assurances. When she had walked down the aisle toward him, her face was set in a grimace so fierce that he had nearly hidden behind the minister. Did she really abhor him so, a man she had never met?

And yet when she stood beside him, he could sense something else. She was angry, true, but perhaps almost — afraid?

She did not say a word to him through the wedding breakfast, nor to anyone else for that matter. She simply sat, as stoic as a soldier about to be sent into battle, as though she were waiting for the entire event to be over and done with.

Not that he blamed her for that, at the very least. This

entire affair was so forced, there was nothing at all natural about it, and that very tension pervaded the room.

Eventually, all of the guests blessedly left, and he was standing alone with her at the cusp of the entryway of his — their — country estate.

"Scarlett," he began, turning toward her, but she remained resolutely stiff, looking out after the dirt kicked up by the carriages as they trundled away down his drive. "I gather this is not quite what you had imagined. I—"

"How did you gather that, oh, wise husband?"

He raised an eyebrow at her sarcasm. "By the petulant way in which you have conducted yourself since the moment you walked into the church."

"Excuse me?" Finally, he had her attention. She turned and looked at him with those eyes that had befuddled him so when they caught his during that moment in which he said his vows. They were hazel, as light as the cinnamon pieces running through her hair but with flecks of gold that danced when she had watched him closely as he had spoken the words to her that bound them together for the rest of their lives.

"I said—"

"I heard what you said. Is that any way to speak to your new wife?"

He crossed his arms over his chest. Who did she think she was, to snipe barbs at him so when he had done nothing but do as was expected of him, the same way she had?

"You have hardly uttered a word since you arrived in the village. You certainly have not spoken to *me*. You avoided me until the moment our wedding actually began. And now you are doing your best to push me away. Am I really so repulsive, Scarlett?"

She was silent for a moment, breaking their locked gaze

as she stared out over the glorious gardens sweeping away from the front door, around the drive and out behind the house.

"I do not wish to be married," she said, her words stilted and angry. "Not to you, nor to anyone else."

"Then why did you agree to marry me?"

"I had no other choice. My father deemed this wedding to be, and so be it. It was that or try to make my own way in the world, and as much as I would like to, I simply ... could not. And you? Why agree to marry me, a woman you have never met?"

"I had business to see to, as I always do. I did not have time to meet and properly court a woman. My father was anxious for heirs. He assured me that you were a well-bred woman who would fit well within my life. He may be a cold man, but he has always seen to my best interests and I trusted him in this."

"You trusted your father to find the appropriate women with whom to spend the rest of your life?" She looked at him incredulously, and he shifted from one foot to the other. When she put it like that, it did sound rather idiotic, but at the time it had made sense. His father had told him she was beautiful, from a good family, and with a significant dowry. That had all been true. What he had never mentioned was her temperament.

Hunter was surprised when she was the first to break the ensuing silence.

"You have a beautiful home, at the very least."

"Thank you," he said, resolving to try to be civil with her. He had no wish to spend a life in conflict with his wife. He had enough of that in his day-to-day affairs, which he spent within the House of Lords. "I primarily live in London, but I have always loved Wintervale. It seemed the ideal place to hold the wedding celebrations. The village is lovely at this time of year, and I have known the minister since I was a child."

"You don't spend much time here?"

"Not really," he said with a shrug. "It seems I have too much requiring my attention in London."

"I see," she said, a contemplative look coming over her face, and he wished he could read her thoughts.

"I thought perhaps we could spend a month or so here before returning to London?" he asked. "I know it will be well in advance of the Season but—"

"Go," she said with a wave of her hand.

"Go?" he asked, confusion filling him. "We will travel together when the time comes."

She looked at him now, her hands on her hips. "I will be honest with you, Lord Oxford. I have no wish to go to London. Not in a month, not for the Season. I think I like it here, and here I will stay."

"But—" He desperately rifled through his mind for the right words to say. It would be rather untoward to show up to London without his wife for the entire Season. He must convince her to come, even for a short time. He took a breath. He was sure she would change her mind. She just needed time. "We will discuss it," he finally said, and she quirked up one side of her lips — the first resemblance to a smile he had seen since he'd met her.

"Very well," she said. "Now I wish to remove this monstrosity of a gown. If you will excuse me."

And with that, she turned, calling for her lady's maid. He followed her from a distance, studying her as she walked through Oak Hall, looking one way and then the other until she discovered the staircase at the end of the connecting Stone Hall. She lifted her "monstrosity," which was, in fact, a beautiful pink gown, though a bit frothy for his taste, up from the floor and started up the grand staircase. He followed her with his eyes all the way up, around the balustrade, and down the balcony that hung over the great room beneath, where he stood, wondering what in the hell had just happened.

He didn't see her again. Not through the afternoon, not even for dinner, despite persistent knocks on her door. "I don't feel well," she had called out. And when he tried her door that evening, to determine how she felt and whether she had any interest in a marriage night, it was as he thought.

The door was locked.

1

December, 1813 ~ London

"Spicer? I'm running late, unfortunately, and the House is to sit in but an hour. Is everything prepared?"

"Of course, my lord." Rupert Spicer had been his faithful valet for the past five years, and Hunter didn't know what he would do without him. The man helped him shrug into his coat, and passed him his hat as he ran out the door. It was the last day the House of Lords was to sit before Christmastide. Hunter diligently attended, unlike his father, who had always abhorred what he called the dull and dreary proceedings.

"Three times!" he would thunder at Hunter. "Three times I would have to sit there and listen to the same bill read. I am *done* with it!"

Despite his initial hesitation, Hunter had found that he enjoyed the opportunity to sit within the House, to affect decisions that could make change in the world. There was nothing of consequence to be discussed today, although

Hunter agreed that the recess until March did seem inexplicably long. There was much to be discussed — not only the war with Bony and France, but after his recent visit to the mill and his ensuing horror at what he found there — children not even ten, worked to the bone — there was much to be done.

While he agreed with Sir James Mackintosh on the fact they should move up the next year's sitting date, the man droned on and on without saying much of anything, and Hunter found his mind wandering. Christmastide. Should he stay in London? Should he attend a house party? He had been invited to several. He attended select parties throughout the Season, but unlike many men such as himself, his primary purpose for remaining in London was not so much the social scene but the true reason he was there — the politics. If he did attend a party or some such event, often it was simply to gain the ear of another lord or cabinet minister.

London would be fairly empty at the moment, however. Should he return to his own country home — to Wintervale? Wintervale, where his bride awaited. At least, he assumed so. He hadn't heard from her since he had left in August. He figured his steward would write him a note if she actually *did* leave. Stone had informed him that she visited her mother now and again, their homes being but a couple of hours' journey between. Hunter had never been a particularly attentive lord, but his father had insisted he take over Wintervale, as he and Hunter's mother preferred to remain in London and had many other estates they could escape to if they found the need for time in the country.

By the time Hunter returned to his townhouse that evening — the townhouse he had purchased for his bride, he thought regretfully, having been perfectly happy in his rented rooms — he was still undecided, and after a quick dinner alone, instead of sitting in his library stewing, he picked his hat up off the desk and called for his carriage to be readied once more. He could always find company at White's. He hopped into the carriage and it soon deposited him in front of the Portland stone building on St. James' Street.

He was relieved to enter and find his friend, Lord Wimbledon, awaiting him.

"Wimbledon!" he called, and the man poured another glass of brandy, leaving it awaiting Hunter across the table.

"Oxford," the man greeted him. "I'm surprised to see you here. I thought with the break in Parliament you would be off to see that new wife of yours."

"Yes, well..." Hunter shifted uncomfortably as he took his seat, unsure of how to answer that. He knew his relationship was on the tongues of many of the *ton*, but there was not much he could do about it. His wife hated him, and he had no idea why.

He had tried to get close to her, truly he had. After their wedding, he had attempted to make peace with her, to find a common ground, but she had completely closed herself off to him, and eventually, not wanting to face any further rejection, he had given up and made his way to London.

Hunter had suffered enough rejection in his life. While he looked up to his father and had spent his life learning from the man, anytime he had spoken a word of his own ideals his father had pushed them aside as though they meant nothing. And as for his mother... Hunter couldn't think of another soul on the planet who possessed less compassion or love — even for her children. His father had always told him to toughen up, that he didn't need the love of a woman. But it had created within Hunter a fear of rejection that he never could quite shake. He knew, however, it was much worse for his sister Lavinia, who had to spend much more time in the presence of the marchioness.

And now here he was, facing another woman who wanted nothing to do with him. He'd prefer not to dwell on it. He had enough on his mind as it was. He had hoped for a conventional, cordial relationship, without the need to worry about his wife and whatever it may be that was causing her such vexation. At some point in time, he supposed he would have to deal with it, but for now, he was preoccupied with the concerns of the House. He sighed, noting that Wimbledon still stared at him.

"I look forward to a wonderful break," he said simply, and Wimbledon took what he wanted from that, leaving it be. Hunter lit a cheroot, sat back in his chair, and stewed. What was he supposed to do now?

HE DIDN'T HAVE to wonder for long.

When he walked into this office the next morning, a footman trailing through the door behind him with a tray holding his coffee and pastries, Hunter found a single enve-lope on the surface of his otherwise tidy desk. He cut through the seal to find the scrawl of his steward, a man to whom his father had entrusted the estate for many years now.

LORD OXFORD,

Forgive me for the intrusion; however, I am aware you are currently on recess. Unfortunately, an urgent matter has arisen that requires your attention. There is an issue with the accounts, one that I cannot solve. I have my suspicions as to the cause of the disturbance. While it should be a straightforward solution, we must speak further.

Sincerely,

Mr. Stone

HE SIGHED. That was certainly cryptic. But his decision was made. He supposed he would be returning to Wintervale after all.

~

SCARLETT SMILED as she pulled on her gloves and dipped her head under the stone archway of the young family's home. The cold bit into her uncovered face, but she paid it no mind. Not now, with the cozy cottage's warmth still filling her as the cool air blew a whisper of snow across the yard.

The children were tiny and so lovely, one just a babe, snuggled deep in his mother's arms. Scarlett's smile faded, however, as she looked out across the fields in front of her. The sun was beginning to set, and she could see the dim light of a candle or fire through windows in the distance. This was but one home, and she had many more to visit over the next few days.

She cursed her husband. The Earl of Oxford. So concerned with his great ideals in the House of Lords that he completely neglected his own tenants. Here were people who needed him, who had barely enough to survive. Did he know? Or did he truly not care?

Scarlett untied her horse from the fencepost and hoisted herself up, hiking up her skirts and swinging one leg over the top of him. No one was around to see her, and she hated riding sidesaddle. When she did, she couldn't mount without assistance, she could hardly control the horse, and she hated when the saddle was cinched so tight that the horse seemed uncomfortable. Of course, the odd time when anyone saw her riding as she was now, they were absolutely shocked, but Scarlett didn't overly care. Let them talk. What did her reputation matter, anyhow?

Wintervale had now been home for four months, and Scarlett had to admit that the adjustment hadn't been nearly as difficult as she had initially thought. The servants were lovely and welcoming, and she had enjoyed visiting the tenants and seeing the lands. Someone had to. The steward, while experienced to be sure, cared only about the numbers and nothing about the people. Any time Scarlett had attempted to discuss anything of importance with him, he had pretended to listen for a moment, then quickly waved away her words with a frown of annoyance. Apparently, he was the sort, as most were, who believed women had nothing to offer.

And then there was Nia. A smile lifted Scarlett's lips as she returned to Wintervale. Hunter's sister, Lavinia, had shown up on the doorstep a day after Hunter had returned to London. She had married the neighbor, she told her, and was but a short ride away. Would she mind if she visited Scarlett now and again? At first, Scarlett had resisted. Did she really want the company, day in and day out, of a woman she had met but once — and the sister of her unwanted husband, no less?

But Lavinia had surprised her. She proved intelligent and humorous, and Scarlett began to enjoy her visits more and more. Lavinia abhorred the outdoors and therefore never chose to join Scarlett in a ride or even working in the beautiful grotto within the gardens, but they saw just enough of one another to not become bored with the other's presence. And it was rather nice to have a friend nearby.

Now, as Scarlett shook off her boots, she heard Lavinia round the corner and come into the foyer.

"Scarlett!" she said as she pushed her spectacles back up her slim nose. "Heavens, I was worried about you. I have been here for hours already! Where have you been for so long on such a cold afternoon?"

"Nothing to worry about, Nia," she said, placing a hand on the woman's shoulder as she walked through the foyer, passing the waiting footman her cloak. Lavinia knew the house well, of course, having spent much of her youth there, and made herself perfectly at home. "I was just visiting some tenants, is all."

"That is lovely of you, Scarlett, but I know my brother wouldn't expect you to do that," Lavinia said, biting her lip.

And that was the one and only reason Scarlett sometimes wished Lavinia didn't visit so often — the continual praise of her brother. Scarlett knew she did it on purpose, but she wasn't going to fall for Lavinia's ploys. She had resolved, however, not to speak ill of the man Lavinia loved so much in her presence.

"Of course he wouldn't," she said simply, leading Lavinia into the back drawing room, the one she favored with its bright, cheery striped satin walls and furniture of a yellow that was somewhat between lemon and amber. The best part was the windows overlooking the grotto. "I choose to do so myself."

"That is kind of you," Lavinia said with a smile as she took a seat on the ornately carved rosewood sofa. "Do you know if my brother is returning for Christmastide?"

"I wouldn't know," said Scarlett, sitting across from her on the matching smaller piece. "As you well know, Nia, he and I do not correspond. You would be more inclined to know the answer to that."

"Well, I suggested he come, but really, that is up to you to request, as his wife. Oh, Scarlett, if only you would get to know him. He really is the nicest man, and I am not simply saying that because he is my brother. He is kind and generous, and yes, he can get caught up in his work, but only because he is so passionate about it! And once he loves something, he gives it his all."

"Clearly this marriage is *not* something that he particularly cares for," Scarlett said bitterly.

"You certainly haven't given him any reason to," said Lavinia, leaning forward, her arm on the sofa's Grecian-urn cresting. "All he needs from you, Scarlett, is a word of welcome. Why are you so cold?"

Scarlett sighed. It wasn't the first time Lavinia had brought this up, and she knew it wouldn't be the last, not until she understood where Scarlett was coming from.

Scarlett stood, cup of tea in hand, and walked over to the window, looking out into the black of the fallen night.

"Let me tell you a story, Nia," she said, as a log cracked in the hearth. "When my mother married my father, she was hopelessly in love with him. He had courted her, and she quickly became infatuated with him. After a typical period of courtship that went entirely as one would expect, they were married in St. George's Cathedral. They consummated the marriage that night, and the day after he was back in the bed of his mistress. My mother didn't learn of this until much later, and when she did, her heart was completely broken."

She had heard Lavinia gasp behind her at her mention of a mistress, and Scarlett turned around to face her, intent with her need for Lavinia to understand.

"My mother loved my father with all of her heart, and he wanted only her dowry. She has lived her life in love with a man who wants nothing from her but to produce heirs, and even in that she failed him, having only me. I will never fall into that trap. I may be married, but as long as I live separate from your brother, I have my freedom. I can do as I please and never have to worry about becoming trapped by my own fickle emotions."

As Lavinia looked at her in shock, Scarlett felt almost guilty for sharing such morbid thoughts with her, but at least now she knew.

"That is the saddest story I have ever heard," Lavinia said, dropping her eyes, so like her brother's but behind spectacles, to her lap. "But you must know that it doesn't have to be like that, Scarlett. My brother is not that kind of man."

Scarlett shrugged, her gaze wandering over the gilt Chippendale carvings that stood out prominently on the walls. "So you may think. My father is also a wonderful man to most that he meets. He is charming, he is kind, he provides for others. Despite the fact he wanted a son so badly, he loves me and has done all he can to provide for me. But my mother is nothing to him. Simply a woman who dresses up and accompanies him to balls. That is not the life for me, Nia, not at all."

"I wish you didn't think like that," Lavinia said sorrowfully, and Scarlett returned to her seat and reached across the small table between them to take Lavinia's hands in her own.

"That doesn't change how happy I am to have you as a sister," she said softly. "I am so glad we became friends."

"Well, on that, Scarlett, we are agreed."

2

Scarlett eyed the candle that sat atop the small yet elegant mahogany table next to her. The wick was burning dangerously low. Would she have enough to finish this last chapter and still be able to return to her room? She could get up and find another, true, but she was rather comfortable at the moment with the huge quilt thrown over her as she snuggled deeper into the depths of the navy bergère chair in the corner of the library.

She tried to make out the time on the mantel clock overtop one of the room's three fireplaces, in which just the embers burned low in the grate, the marble chimney stretching far above it. As hard as she squinted, however, she couldn't quite read it in the dark, though if she had to guess, she would assume it was just past midnight. A time when the rest of the house was asleep, of course. Lavinia had departed for home after dinner, and the servants were now all abed. Scarlett always prepared for sleep early so that Marion, her maid, didn't have to wait up for her, but then she would sneak back down to the library. She had never been one to sleep early or even overly much. If she did go to bed at what others would consider a proper time, she would spend the night tossing and turning, and so she usually read until her eyes felt heavy enough to promise sleep.

One thing she did have to commend her husband on was the depths of his bookshelves. They were filled with tomes of every sort, from gothic novels to histories to children's books. Lavinia told her that all of the books from their London home and her parents' second country estate were sent here when her mother decided to redecorate. They were supposed to have been collected and returned, but her mother decided to instead buy books that "looked like they belonged." Whatever that meant, thought Scarlett with an eye roll.

She was currently reading a hidden treasure she had found the other day, a history of Wintervale. The first stone had been laid in March of 1650, a fact that had apparently been gleaned from a diary. That, she would have to find as well. Why she was so interested in the family of a man from whom she was doing all she could to distance herself, she had no idea, but she would love to know more of the people who graced the paintings on the walls and who had walked the very floorboards she now haunted herself.

She was reading about the third earl. It was a romantic story. He was originally rejected as a suitor by his initial prospective father-in-law, as the earl was in rather ill health. His friends arranged another marriage for him, and when he met this woman on his wedding day, he instantly fell in love with her; they had two sons and a wonderful life together.

"Hmph." Scarlett closed the book. Did she trust this romantic portrayal, or was it simply a fairy tale?

She leaned her head back on the cushion behind her. There was a chance it might be true. But that didn't mean love was worth the risk — at least, not for her.

HUNTER EASED OPEN the door as he let himself into the house. While he hadn't been able to see the familiar red brick in the darkness of night, when he stepped into the entrance hall, the home welcomed him like a mother with open arms. Well, like most mothers would. With the exception of his own.

He had always loved this house, and he hadn't realized how much he had missed it until he had neared it. If only his bride would welcome him, then perhaps he could begin to spend more time here once again, at least when Session was out.

Spicer, his valet, had gone around the back and said he would prepare everything within his chamber before Hunter went up to bed. He was tired — it had been a long trip from London — but he decided a glass of brandy wouldn't hurt to warm him up some after the frigid air that had made its way into the carriage and through the wrapper around him on the journey here.

He and Lavinia had always preferred this home, and once they were old enough, they chose to spend most of their time here as opposed to the cold, stately home their parents currently occupied and preferred. The oak floorboards creaked under his weight as he strode down the foyer and Oak Hall. He made his way through the Green Room, turning left around the inner courtyard until he came to the room that was always home to him — his library. He was surprised when he pushed open the door and found the room warm, the embers in one of the hearths still lit as though the fire had just died out. Had someone been in here — his wife, perhaps? He made his way over through the dim yet familiar room to find the decanter of brandy just where it always was and he poured himself a drink. Eyes half closed, he meandered around the furniture to find his favorite chair, the one that knew his body better than any woman ever would.

Seeing the quilt his grandmother had made for him already draped over the chair, it was as though it had been waiting for him. Nothing was quite like coming home.

He bent and sat down, letting out a shout as something moved beneath him.

The body emitted a yelp of its own, before coming off the chair faster than he could have ever anticipated, barreling into him with the ferocity of England's best wrestler.

"What in the hell?" he shouted as his drink went flying, spilling its amber liquid all over the Aubusson carpet as he came down with a thud beside it. But he was currently more worried about the wildcat atop of him.

"Who are you, you brute?" it yelled, and it took Hunter a moment to recognize the voice. He had heard it before, though not often. It was the anger behind it that allowed familiarity to sink in.

"Scarlett!" he yelled out as he attempted to grab hold of her wrists to keep her from continuing to pummel him. "It's me, your — your husband!"

"My who?" She sounded a bit confused but sat back on her heels, and he took the opportunity to come to his knees and shuffle back, out of her reach.

"Your husband," he repeated, more calmly now. "Hunter."

She stood then, making a hasty retreat away from him. "What — what are you doing here?" she asked in confusion.

"Well, this is my home," he said dryly. "I should be able to come here anytime I wish without fear of being beaten to death."

"You came upon me in the middle of the night with no word of warning!" she protested. "You could have been anyone. How was I to know that you would decide to return home after darkness, prowling about like a thief?"

"You seem to be forgetting that this is my library, *wife*," he said. "I can come and go as I please. If you ever deigned to write me, perhaps you would learn more of my movements."

Not that he himself had known he would be here until this morning, but it wasn't as though he was going to share that information with her. She had chosen to distance herself from him, so any lack of communication was solely on her.

"You never told Lavinia," she accused, and he didn't need light to know that a smug smile had crossed her face.

"No, I did not," he said dryly, looking for a match and lantern in the darkness. "Nor do I need my sister's approval. I am the master of this house, am I not?"

"That is what I am told, though I have yet to see you act as one," she said, and he took a deep breath to wrest hold of his temper.

"Is that not what you wanted? For me to remain in London?"

"It is."

"Then don't pester me about it, Scarlett," he said.

"Lady Oxford."

"You are my wife, so Scarlett you shall be."

They were both silent for a moment as he finally found a match and lit the lantern, though she was far enough from him that he could only see the shadows of her face. They were at an impasse, it seemed.

"You have been making yourself comfortable," he remarked, now trying to ignore the way her body looked, silhouetted by the dim light. She was wearing nothing but a nightgown, her thin wrapper currently hanging off one arm after their struggles. She must have seen him staring, for she began to hastily pull her other sleeve back up. In his pent-up frustration toward her, he had forgotten how alluring she was. She had curves in all of the right places, her body tempting him to dismiss the words that came out of her mouth. But then she spoke and the tension came rushing back in.

"Your house is quite comfortable, Lord Oxford, I must admit," she said, tilting her head. "'Tis a pity you neglect it."

"Hunter."

She said nothing.

He sighed and ran a hand through his hair. Unable to stand there staring at her any longer, he picked up his glass and returned to the sideboard to pour himself another.

"I am unsure of what I have done to hold such low esteem with you, Scarlett," he said, his back to her. "But you are my wife, and there is nothing you can do to change that fact now. Can we not find some sort of peace between us?"

She looked down at the ground, where the stain was beginning to spread over the carpet.

"We need to clean this," she murmured, apparently choosing to ignore his words. She walked over to him, knelt down by his feet, and before he could ask what in the blazes she was doing, she began to rummage around through the cupboard's contents until she found what she was looking for.

"Here we are," she said, pulling out a piece of fabric. How had she known where to find it? She returned to the carpet and began to blot out the liquid.

"Let me help you," he said, putting down his glass, though not before taking a gulp of the brandy, letting it burn its way down his throat.

"It's fine, I've got it," she said, but he dismissed her resistance, taking one of the pieces of cloth in hand and beginning to blot out the liquid with her. He moved when she did, and their hands brushed against one another. He was startled by the jolt of heat that shot through him. He sat back on his haunches and looked at her, but her gaze remained rooted on the floor. Was her hand shaking slightly? He quickly shook his head, dismissing the notion.

Now that he was closer, he could better make out her features. He had nearly forgotten what she looked like, their time together having been so brief while their separation so long. He could see the smattering of freckles over her nose, though much of her face was hidden by the long curtain of her deep brown hair, which hung straight and loose around her shoulders.

If only she hadn't built such a wall around herself, he thought with resignation. How very different this time together could be.

"That should do it," she said abruptly, gathering the cloth and placing it by the door. "Your Aubusson is saved."

"Thank you for your noble deed, my lady," he said with a slight bow in jest, but she only raised an eyebrow at him.

"I will be to bed then," she said.

She turned to the door, but he called out to her before

she could go too far. "Scarlett?" She stopped. "Why are you awake at such a late hour?"

"I cannot sleep," she said with a shrug. "I have never been able to."

And neither could he. Perhaps they were more alike than either of them realized.

3

"Hunter, you're home!"

Scarlett didn't think she had ever see Lavinia so animated as when she ran through the door of the dining room, stopping with her skirts still billowing around her as she looked about in bewilderment for her brother.

Her face fell when she found only Scarlett sitting there.

"I heard Hunter was home," she said by way of apology, sitting down at the table. Scarlett shrugged. "Apparently he did not wake in time for breakfast," she said, but her comment was slightly presumptuous as the man in question strolled into the room. Lavinia stood up from the table so abruptly that her Chippendale chair went flying backward. She ran the few steps remaining between them and all but jumped into her brother's arms.

"Oh, Hunter, it is so wonderful to see you! I was asking Scarlett just yesterday if she knew whether you were going to grace us with your presence this Christmastide. Isn't it lovely Scarlett?"

Scarlett forced a smile onto her face. If nothing else, it

was wonderful to see Hunter's sister so joyful. Scarlett swallowed the piece of toast that was stuck in her throat, momentarily unsure of what to say. For she had forgotten how devastatingly handsome Hunter was, but now that he stood here before her in the light of day, she found herself reminded. Last night after she had tackled him to the floor, when he looked at her she felt the intensity of his gaze, but in the dim light she hadn't been able to appreciate the true allure of his blue-green eyes, which she now remembered much more vividly as the sun streamed in through the window to descend on the masculine planes of his face.

He and Lavinia were alike in coloring, but that was where the similarities ended. Where she was round, he was angular, and where she was soft, he was hard muscle. Scarlett hadn't paid near enough attention to their parents to notice which they favored, but she seemed to recall the marquess reminding her of his son.

"Where is that husband of yours?"

"Oh, you know Baxter," she said with a wave of her hand. "He had some business or other to attend to" —likely a cheroot and a newspaper, if Scarlett knew well enough— "but said he would be by to see you later on. We will be spending much time together over Christmas, I'm sure."

"I, ah, I'm not sure how long I will be staying."

"What?" Lavinia's joy evaporated suddenly. "You only just arrived, Hunter, and Christmas is but days away. You must stay. Please, say you will. We will have dinner together, and we are even hosting a New Year's Eve party. It will be great fun."

"We shall see," he said noncommittally, before raising his head to look directly at Scarlett. "Good morning, Scarlett."

"Lord Oxford."

"Hunter."

"Well," Lavinia said after a moment of silence, while she looked back and forth between them. "I think I should probably go. I'm sure the two of you have much to discuss."

"Please stay," Scarlett said, trying to keep the desperation out of her voice. "In fact, we actually saw one another last night when Hunt— Lord Oxford arrived, so there is no need for you to go."

"Last night? I was here until well past dinner. What time did you get in, Hunter?" Lavinia asked.

"Just after midnight."

"Oh!" Lavinia's cheeks reddened as she mistakenly assumed the nature of their meeting. "Then you— that's wonderful! Well, not that I should be saying a thing, I simply hoped — well..."

Scarlett saved her from her rambling. "Lord Oxford and I scarcely said hello, Nia. I was reading in the library and Lord Oxford ... happened upon me."

"I see," she said, an eyebrow still raised. "Well, ah, yes, I should be going then. Goodbye!"

And then with a flounce of her skirts, she was gone, leaving the two of them to stare at one another awkwardly.

Hunter cleared his throat and walked to the sideboard, loading a plate with ham, eggs, and toast. He poured himself a coffee and sat down across from Scarlett, who simply watched him. He moved gracefully, despite his height and solid frame. She watched as he buttered his bread and stirred sugar into his coffee before lifting the cup to his mouth.

"See something interesting?" he asked, and she jumped, startled out of her reverie.

Good Lord, Scarlett, get it together. This was the last thing she wanted — to be inexplicably attracted to the man she

28

was trying so hard to distance herself from. What if she came too close, if she not only developed feelings for him beyond attraction, but eventually fell in love with him? Unfortunately, she knew all too well what the end result would be. He would be back in London, the city she hated, living his life alone, free from her, while she pined away here at Wintervale, her previous enjoyable life now filled with despair.

"Nothing at all," she finally drawled back, hopeful that he didn't notice how nervous she was. She needed to get out of here. She placed her hands on the table to push back her chair, but he held up a finger to halt her.

"Scarlett," he said, playing with her name. "There is something we must discuss. Something that Lavinia touched upon."

"Yes?"

"You have made it clear you want little to do with me. However, the fact of the matter is, we are married, and I am in line to become a marquess one day. We need children, Scarlett, you must realize that."

She swallowed hard. She shouldn't be surprised by his words. As he said, they were married, and that was what was expected. And yet, the thought of him in her bed ... well, actually the thought of him in her bed was not altogether an unpleasant one, and that is what scared her the most.

"I think ... there are a few things we must first determine before it comes to that," she said, doing her best to maintain her composure.

"And those would be?" He raised an eyebrow and leaned back in his chair. His curls were haphazardly skewed around his head, and Scarlett felt a strange urge to lean forward and run her hands over them, but, of course, she restrained herself.

"Where would we raise said children? You spend all of your time in London, and I have no wish to live there."

"What's wrong with London?"

"It's so ... dirty," she said, which was partly the truth. "Everyone is so close together all the time, and there is no freedom."

"You value your freedom," he observed.

"I do," she said, leaning forward. "More than you know."

"Very well," he said, waving a hand out in front of him. "Raise them here. I enjoy Wintervale and will come home as often as possible."

"As you have these past few months?"

"Come, Scarlett, that is hardly fair. You all but pushed me from the house."

She looked down at her plate. He was right. She had been an absolute fiend to him. In trying to protect herself, she had made him believe that she was a monster, one he couldn't even live with. Whatever was she to do?

Despite feeling like a coward, she chose not to respond to his last statement.

"If you do not want to even stay for Christmas, then why did you come?" she eventually asked.

"My steward tells me there are matters that I must attend to. Urgent matters, actually. I should likely find him post-haste."

"Mr. Stone?" She allowed disdain to drip from her words. "Is there anything I can do to help?"

"To help? With what?" he asked as he stood, looking down at her with confusion.

"With the estate. I have done all I can to try to improve things while you were gone. In fact, I should like to speak with you about a few matters of importance."

"Oh?" He looked down at her, still bemused, but finally a

small smile crossed his lips. "I am glad you are enjoying running the household, Scarlett, truly I am. It has been some time since anyone has called Wintervale home for more than a month at a time. I'm sure the staff appreciates having you here. Well, I will be off now. We will talk again later on this evening."

And then he was walking out the door, leaving Scarlett to stare at his back. She hadn't meant running the household, not at all. Mrs. Shepherd did a well enough job of that, and Scarlett left her to it. Apparently, it hadn't occurred to Hunter that his wife might have a thought to the estate itself. He certainly had neglected it, and Stone was completely incompetent, so someone had to do it. Well, he would find out her thoughts soon enough.

"SHE WHAT?"

Hunter rose from the chair behind his wide mahogany desk, rounding it to stare at his steward. The man looked up at him with a satisfied expression, his smile marred by his untidy teeth. He seemed pleased with Hunter's reaction, which irked him all the more.

"Yes, my lord, she's been giving away the money! And for nothing. Just handing it to people, like 'here ya go,' with them doing nothing for it! I told her time and again not to, but she told me, she's the countess, and I'm the steward, so what am I to do? That's why I sent for you, my lord, so you could hopefully talk some sense into her."

Hunter paused for a moment, staring down at his knuckles grinding into his desk, before walking around it and beginning to pace. This was why he had a capable steward — so he didn't have to worry about these matters at home. He was preoccupied, trying to affect change throughout the country. There were children working harder than grown men in mills, men and women in prisons and asylums being treated worse than animals. He should be working to pass bills that would impact the lives of many. But no, instead he now had to see to his wife, who decided to quench the boredom of remaining here in the country by involving herself in things she knew nothing about.

"How do you know this?" he asked with some resignation, accepting what Stone was telling him.

"There's been money missing for a couple of months now, my lord. I tried to ascertain where it had gone but found nothing amiss. There was but one account it was coming from — the one your wife is able to access. At first, I thought she was spending it on frivolous things, like dresses and the like, but then I heard a rumor round the village of people who were better off than they were before. I confronted her about it, and she didn't even bother to hide it!"

Well, at the very least, his wife was honest, that was for certain.

"I think this could lead to some very nasty surprises, my lord," Stone continued, his voice practically dripping with hatred. "Imagine some folks having more than others. They'll say the earl and his wife are playing favorites. Soon enough she'll be wanting them all to pay lower rates — ha!"

Hunter sighed and ran a hand through his hair. He had never had the patience for this sort of thing. He didn't want to be here counting figures and dissolving tensions. He much preferred a good, upfront argument between gentlemen, as he pushed for needed change. But, here he was. His father had given him this land with the understanding that he would take care of it, and that he must do. Even if it meant pushing his wife even further away.

"I suppose I best go speak with her," he said, dismissing his steward, who nodded at him, a smug smile on his face as he departed.

Hunter's study was, conveniently he supposed, near his wife's bedroom and sitting area. It was still mid-morning, and he was sure he would find her there. What she did with her time, he wasn't sure, but likely the typical embroidery, or perhaps she was waiting for a neighbor to call. That was what most ladies did, anyway.

He didn't realize how much of a surprise he was in for.

4

His wife was nowhere to be found. Not in her own chambers, in any of the drawing rooms, or even the kitchen or servant areas. Hunter searched every part of the house.

"Ah, Mrs. Shepherd!" he called, seeing the housekeeper bustle from one room to the next.

She paused her ample frame to look at him. "Yes, my lord?"

"Have you seen my wife?"

"No, my lord," she said, but then added, "Have you looked out over the grounds?"

"Outdoors?" he asked, wondering if the housekeeper was confused.

"Yes, my lord," she said with a nod. "Her ladyship, she likes to ride, enjoys being out in the grotto, even in winter, or riding through the trees just beyond the gardens. You can often find her there. In fact, if you take the stairs and look through one of the upper windows, you might catch a glimpse of her. That's where I always look for her first."

Hunter stared after the middle-aged woman in some

amusement before shrugging and doing as she said. He looked out the window to the east and south, and sure enough, there she was, striding toward the stable. He couldn't make out her features from here, but certainly no one else with long, unruly chestnut hair billowing in the wind, a cloak stretched out behind her, would be headed toward the stables on this winter day.

She was certainly leading him on a chase. He ran down the stairs, fetching his own cloak before continuing out the front entrance and across the yard, following her footprints in the snow. Where had she been coming from? What was she doing out here?

He entered the barn just as she was mounting her horse.

"Scarlett!" he called. "Hold on a minute. I have to speak to you."

He came up short when he stood in front of her. He looked up at her in astonishment before turning his face to the groom, whose cheeks burned from more than the cold as he looked away from the two of them to the floor.

"What do you think you are doing? And what are you wearing?"

"A riding habit," she said, as though he were daft. "And breeches."

"You cannot ride around like that!"

"Why not?" she asked, leaning over her horse's head to peer down at him. "Men ride around in breeches all the time. And when I arrive where I need to be, I simply shake my skirts down over my legs. Hardly anyone sees me ride, and no one knows the difference. Do you know how much faster one can ride astride in comparison to sidesaddle? How less dangerous it is? Why I could never ride alone if I were draped over the side like a sack of potatoes!"

"You *shouldn't* be riding alone! I... I..."

He was at a loss for words. He brought his hand to his forehead. "Never mind that for now. There is an urgent matter we must discuss."

"It seems most things are urgent with you, Lord Oxford."

"Hunter. Yes, well, will you just come down, please? My neck hurts from looking up at you."

"I am going on a ride. My horse needs exercise, as do I. We can speak later."

"We really must speak now. I—"

But his words were lost in the air that flew by him as she urged her horse into a gallop and swept out of the stable, right past him. He stood there for a moment, staring after her in shock, before turning to his groom.

"Best ready my horse," he said with resignation.

SCARLETT LAUGHED as she eased back on Star's reins, slowing her horse slightly. Oh, but teasing Hunter was much more fun than she had expected. She could tell he had no idea what to do with her, and that was all very well. She also had a suspicion of what he wanted to speak to her about, seeing as he had been in his study for part of the morning already, meeting with the ghastly Stone. The man was a nightmare, and in fact, she did want to speak to Hunter about getting rid of him, amongst other things.

She hadn't lied about needing the exercise, for her or the horse. Scarlett loved the freedom riding provided her, and she always allowed her hair free of its ties, today flowing from underneath her fur cap. When she opened her eyes once more, she knew she was not alone, and she looked over at Hunter, who had nearly pulled even with her.

"Impressive, Lord Oxford," she called out. "I had quite the head start."

"Yes, well, apparently you slowed," he responded. "Though why, heaven only knows."

"You simply have to ask me, Lord Oxford," she said. "In fact, there are some things I should like to speak with you about as well. I thought we would be better off out here, away from everything and everyone, than in close quarters."

"Very well," he said, suspicion in his tone, but before responding to him, Scarlett looked around them to see they had made it to a clearing in the trees. The evergreens circled them, with one break in the trees that allowed for a view out onto the rest of the land beyond. The ground was currently snow-covered, the trees in the distance blanketed in the snow that had fallen the night before. The morning was warm, however, and Scarlett only hoped the snow would remain until after Christmas. Somehow, it always felt more like a true Christmas when the earth was covered in white.

After dismounting, she turned to find Hunter standing against his horse, arms crossed over his chest as he waited for her to speak. She took a breath. She didn't enjoy conflict — normally she simply avoided it — but this needed to be said.

"It's about your tenants, Lord Oxford," she said, noting his nostrils flare at her words. "They are not well off, not at all. Many of them are poor and hungry, despite the fact that they seem to be successful in what they are growing and the animals they are raising. You own all this land," she said, extending her arms in a wide circle around them, "for miles, and yet you do nothing for it. You leave others to do the work for you, while you simply collect their pay. It's not fair, Lord Oxford, especially when you are making them pay exorbitant figures for rent."

His frown deepened as she spoke, his stance as frigid as the air around them.

"Are you questioning the way I treat my people? Do you really think I would be so harsh with them?"

She stepped toward him, finger pointed into his chest. "Yes, I am questioning you, and of course I think that way! I have seen it myself. Over the last few months, while you have been busy with your lords in London, I have been here, visiting them, seeing firsthand how they live and the way they are struggling. You know nothing of it! At least, I hope you are simply ignorant, for if this is purposeful, then I am even more horrified than I ever could have imagined."

She was breathing hard, and she noted he was doing the same, as she could feel the rise and fall of his chest underneath the tip of her finger, which was now pressed into his cloak.

"Do you have any idea, Scarlett, of what I have been doing in London, to try to make lives better for the very people you are accusing me of sending into dire straits? No, you don't. Have I visited my tenants lately? No. But only because you have been here, keeping me away. Do not accuse me of not caring for them. I have a very capable steward in place who looks after them while I am away. And while we are on the subject, I must speak to you about the fact that you seem to be taking matters into your hands, giving these people money that you have no authority to give!"

"If I could have the money for dresses or furniture for this grand house, then why can I not spend it where I see fit for a much better purpose?"

"Because that is not the way of things!" he burst out, raising his hands into the air. "You're supposed good deeds will only lead to people feeling like they have been treated unfairly, that you are favoring some of them over others."

"If that is seriously what you think, Hunter," she said, not noticing until it rolled off her tongue that she had slipped and used his given name, "then you know nothing at all."

They stood there in tableau, staring at one another, until finally he sighed, running his gloved hand through his hair as he turned from her to look out onto the land beyond. He placed his hands on his hips and tipped his head back, as though he were deep in thought. He finally turned back to her.

"Fine, Scarlett," he said, "We will go visit the tenants and determine if it is as you say."

"Truly?" she asked, raising an eyebrow at him.

"Yes," he said with a shrug. "I should visit them at Christmastide, anyway."

"And your steward," she said, stepping toward him once more. "He has to go."

Hunter scoffed. "I am not getting rid of Stone. He has been with the family for years and is quite capable."

"Have you looked at the books lately?"

"No, but—"

"Do you know what he is charging for rents?"

"Of course."

"Tell me."

"I don't need to tell you anything."

"See, you have no idea. Just look."

"Fine, Scarlett," he said, raising his hands in the air. "I do not know the current rents. Are you happy now?"

"Somewhat," she replied, turning to walk back to her horse, anger still simmering in her belly. She was frustrated in his inability to see what was right in front of his face, while he put his faith in people who had no business in having it. And yet he questioned *her*!

As she returned to Star, Scarlett noted the way the snow was crunching under her feet. It had become wet and sticky with the warmer air of the morning. A smile crossed her face as she knelt down and gathered some of it in her gloved hands, packing it together.

She took a quick look behind her to see Hunter standing there, looking off in the distance with a thoughtful expression on his face. Ah, so maybe some of her words had actually gotten through his thick skull. Well, if they didn't, then hopefully this would. She turned, and, as quickly as she could, launched the ball of snow through the air, before it came down on its mark, hitting him square in the chest.

He let out a shout as he turned to her, his face aghast as though he couldn't believe what she had just done.

And she laughed. Oh, it felt good to find that release, to be able to send some of her frustration flying toward him through the snow. But then his mouth settled in a firm line and he narrowed his eyes at her, and she took a long swallow. Had she gone too far?

But then, quicker than she could have imagined, he knelt himself, scooped up the snow and launched a ball of it at her, the snow exploding over her cloak and dress beneath. Pieces of it broke off and began to melt on the exposed skin of the top of her chest and neck above her chemisette.

"You ... you ... scoundrel!" she finally shrieked, but he just laughed at her words. His laugh was loud and booming, and she realized it was the first time she had heard it. Not that she had given him much opportunity to find anything humorous around her.

"Do not give out what you cannot take back in equal measure, Scarlett!" he called out to her, and then with a shout she was balling up the snow again, as was he. It seemed no sooner did she launch one projectile at him that he was sending one back her way. She threw with all her might, though she knew he was keeping some force back from her. She crowed with exhilaration when she saw he took a direct hit to the face, and he let out a holler.

"Careful, now, wife," he growled, though he wore a smile to go along with it. "You will get yourself into more trouble than you can take."

"We shall see about that!" she said, and she bent to pick up another. When she stood, however, he was gone, and she whipped her head one way and the other trying to find him. But where did he— she let out a piercing scream as suddenly her entire back was wet with icy snow, and she turned to find him behind her, satisfaction on his face as he took in her expression.

"I told you to watch yourself," he said with a wink and a wicked grin.

She didn't think then, not of how she was trying to keep her distance nor that he was much stronger than she and this could not end well for her. She simply launched herself at him, taking him off guard and the two of them went flying backward into the snow.

Scarlett tackled him with frustration, but with laughter as well. And then she raised herself up from him and caught his gaze — and suddenly, with his twinkling blue-green eyes staring up at her, losing some of their humor and becoming altogether serious, nothing seemed funny any longer.

5

_____

Hunter swallowed hard.

Scarlett's face was but inches from his, so close that he could count every freckle covering her pert nose. He knew the moment everything changed, when her eyes widened and she took her plump bottom lip between her crooked front teeth.

He could feel every inch of her body on top of him. She was soft in some places, hard and lithe in others. Despite lying in a pile of snow, Hunter felt no cold at all; rather he was heated down to his very bones.

Trying not to scare her away, he slowly, carefully, lifted his head, closing the space between them. He kept her stare, encouraging her to stay with him, but the moment his lips were but a breath away from hers, she scrambled back away from him, her hands and knees biting into him in her haste to retreat.

"I'm sorry," she said, her words coming out in a rush of breath. "I shouldn't have done that. I—"

"It's all right," he said, waving a hand at her as he stood, brushing the snow off of his cloak and trousers. "Just a bit of fun."

"I know. I shouldn't have—"

"Stop apologizing, Scarlett," he said, coming up behind her and helping to clear the snow from her own cloak. He wasn't sure what she was apologizing for — the fact that she broke away from him, that she took him down in the first place, or that she had even started this game. "It's fine."

She said nothing, turning away from him with her careful facade back in place, hiding all emotion. He sighed. Why did she turn from him so? If only he knew what was keeping her away, then perhaps he could help fix it. Unless it was simply him. For the last thing he wanted was to be dismissed for who he was. Finally he had come to a place in his life where he had found purpose, when people accepted him for the person he was, for the attitudes he held and the work he did. He had suffered enough rejection in his early life. He didn't need it from his wife.

Hunter watched her as she walked over to her horse. She gently rubbed the stallion's nose, whispering soft words into his ear, too quiet for Hunter to hear. In this moment of vulnerability, when she had her guard down, he had the chance to simply look at her. And she was heart-stopping. Her breath was like smoke in front of her face in the cool air, the sun glinting reddish-gold highlights off her hair, which had come loose from its pins on top of her head and was now floating around her face, moving softly with the slight whisper of wind. She was a winter nymph, and he wished he could know this side of her more intimately.

As though sensing his stare, she whirled around and the wall came up once more, shuttering her from his view.

"We should go," she said, and as he walked over to help her mount, she launched herself upon the horse all on her own, hiking up her skirt. Those damn breeches,

43

thought Hunter. They let him see every inch of her shapely legs, made his mind wander to places it had no business being.

"So we should," he muttered, and, feeling completely useless, walked back to his own horse as she kicked her heels in and began the trek home.

She may confuse the hell out of him, but never in his life had Hunter witnessed a woman who could ride as Scarlett did. Nor most men, were he being honest. She and her mount were like one, not only in their movements but in the way her hair seemed to be an extension of the horse's mane, the chestnut hue of the horse a perfect match for his wife's coloring. She was exhilarating. And wanted nothing to do with him, that much was clear.

"WELCOME HOME, MY LORD," Henry Abbot, the butler at Wintervale for as long as Hunter could remember, greeted him as he arrived.

"Abbot," he said, nodding to the man. "How fares the household today?"

"Very well, my lord, very well," he said. "And may I say, my lord, how happy we all are to have you home."

"Thank you, Abbot," he said, then looking from side to side to ensure no one — particularly his wife, who told him she would be staying in the stables for a few more minutes with her horse — was nearby, he questioned his butler. "Abbot, I'd like to ask you ... how does the staff feel about Lady Oxford? Is she fair? Has she treated you well?"

He hadn't given it a thought until now, and he felt some guilt that he had left so abruptly months prior without determining whether his staff would fare well under his wife's direction. If she were so cold and standoffish with him, what was she like to the rest of them?

"Lady Oxford? Oh, she is wonderful, my lord," Abbot said with such admiration and enthusiasm that Hunter nearly took a step back in shock. "All of the staff love her, my lord. She is very kind, and generous too. We see to whatever she may need, of course, but she is always concerned about our wellbeing. When Cook was burned, my lady saw to the wound herself, she did! And when it was discovered one of the maids was with child — not that we want to speak much of that, of course — my lady ensured she was well looked after. When there were complications, she told her to take time away, with pay. Oh, yes, my lord, we like her very much."

"I see," murmured a surprised Hunter. "Thank you, Abbot."

The butler nodded and walked away with Hunter's cloak over his arm, leaving Hunter to stare after him. What did everyone else see that he didn't?

"AND THEN, Marion, I just lay there on top of him as though I were a blathering idiot, an infatuated, flirting tease! What was I thinking?" Scarlett laid her chin in her hands as she looked in the mirror of her vanity table. Her lady's maid scampered about the room behind her, laying out her clothing for dinner. Scarlett had removed all of her wet garments and now sat with her wrapper around her as she warmed herself with a cup of tea after her romp in the snow. She had nearly allowed Hunter to kiss her. She had to be more careful. The man said himself that he would be off to London soon, and if she allowed herself to feel anything for him, here she would sit, pining away for him like some lovesick young girl.

That, she would not allow to happen.

"Perhaps, Marion, I should go visit my mother for Christmas. I haven't seen her in over a month now, and you know how she loves Christmas so."

Marion stepped back from Scarlett's wardrobe to look at her in the mirror. She had been with Scarlett since she was a girl, had practically grown up with her. Scarlett knew how untoward it was to share such confidence with a maid, but besides Lavinia — who, as Hunter's sister, she couldn't completely take into her confidence about certain matters — she had no one else to speak to. Marion had proven time and again she could be trusted, and Scarlett appreciated their closeness.

"It's not for me to say, really, Lady Scarlett," she said, scratching her head underneath her mob cap. "Though if I had a husband who looked like yours, I wouldn't stray far."

"Marion!" Scarlett's head snapped up and she turned to look at her maid with astonishment. "I can hardly believe—"

"Forgive me, my lady, that was not right for me to say, not at all," Marion said, her cheeks flushed.

"It's fine," Scarlett said with a wave of her hand. "I was taken aback, that's all. You know how I feel about letting him in too close."

She flipped open the locket around her neck, taking in the miniature of her mother, who looked so like the reflection that was staring back at her. Scarlett loved her mother beyond words. She was kind and beautiful, inside and out, with so much love to give. Her father had cast that aside, and Lady Halifax had schooled Scarlett to protect herself from the same circumstances. She told her daughter she never wanted her to suffer such hurt.

"The staff has talked about him, before, Lady Scarlett, and I must say ... he doesn't seem that bad a sort. Perhaps if you gave him an opportunity—"

"No, Marion," she said, harsher than she intended, and she softened her words with a smile. "Besides, if he leaves in a couple of days as he plans to, then it doesn't much matter, now does it?"

"I suppose not."

Marion helped her into a simple but beautiful, flowing red dress, with an empire waist and cap sleeves, before draping a shawl around her shoulders.

Marion cleared her throat. "I don't suppose ... never mind."

"What is it?" Scarlett asked, turning to look at her, surprised to see Marion's eyes on the ground as she scuffed her toe into the carpet.

"I was wondering — do you know anything of Lord Oxford's valet? Mr. Spicer? But no, of course you don't. Why would he speak to you of his valet? Forget I asked. Off you go, now."

Scarlett grinned, pleased to have a distraction from her own musings. "Why, Marion? Do you happen to have a penchant for this Mr. Spicer?" She couldn't picture the man in her head, but then, she had little cause to note her husband's valet.

"No! Yes. Oh, my lady, he is awfully handsome. He caught my eye at the time of your wedding, if I were being honest, and then of course I didn't see him again until just this week. I simply wondered whether he was a single man, that is all."

"That, Marion, I can find out," she said, with purpose

now, and Marion smiled gratefully. Interesting, though Scarlett. She wasn't sure how well it could potentially work out between the two of them, but Marion was a grown woman and could choose her own actions.

"Wait!" Marion called as Scarlett made to leave. "One more thing."

She came up beside Scarlett, fastening small diamonds hanging from wires to her ears.

"Earrings? Oh Marion, I'm not sure—"

"They're small and tasteful, and they look lovely on you," said Marion. "Have a wonderful dinner."

Scarlett let out a little snort but allowed Marion to send her on her way like a doting mother. If she didn't know any better, she would think Marion was trying to push her together with her husband. But her maid knew her far better than that to think such a ploy might work — didn't she?

6

Hunter ran a hand through his hair as he tried to concentrate on the numbers in front of him. Despite his protestations to Scarlett, her words resonated with him, and he resolved to determine if what she said had any truth to it. In his study, he found the general ledgers, though he knew Stone would keep the detailed records in his own office.

Nothing seemed untoward, no funds missing, although the overall sum for rents *did* seem slightly high. He would visit his tenants and meet with Stone tomorrow, he decided, for a proper review of the accounts. Then after that, it would be back to London.

But first, dinner with his wife.

His wife. He didn't know what to make of the woman. She was an enigma, and it was rather trying to determine what sort of mood she would be in. One moment she would let her guard down, showing him a side that was warm and inviting. And then the next she would be closed off once more, presenting him with that icy facade. He still wasn't sure what he had done to deserve such treatment, but he was going to find out.

He left his study at the same moment she stepped out of her bedroom down the hall. She didn't see him, not at first, and he took the opportunity to study her side profile. She looked a temptress this evening in her crimson gown, the red shimmering in the glow of the light from the wall sconce. With her defenses down, her vulnerability emerged, the uncertainty etched on her face. It wasn't a side to her he had ever seen before, and as he took her in, she became more human in his eyes and less of a puzzle.

She must have sensed his presence, for suddenly she jumped slightly and turned toward him.

"Lord Oxford," she said with a curtsy.

"If you call me Lord Oxford one more time, I swear I will..."

"You'll what?"

He swallowed hard as suddenly all sorts of delicious punishments came to mind.

"I'll pelt you with another snowball," he finally managed.

"I believe I handled myself just fine earlier today," she retorted but with a smile.

Hunter held out his arm to her, and she took it tentatively. She was lovely, that much was certain, despite the snarl that came from within from time to time. He led her into the dining room, holding out her chair while she sat down gracefully. She was just to his left, his place set at the head of the table. It was slightly more intimate than a typical dinner, and he wondered if they had been placed this way on purpose. His dining room was comfortable, with its carved wall panels, watercolors, and tapestries, and despite the elaborate gilded chandelier and the fact that the room could seat over forty people if they wished, it still felt like the perfect setting for the two of them.

"That is a beautiful locket you wear," he said as their soup course was served.

"Oh, thank you," she said, and he noticed the way she unconsciously caught the necklace between her fingers.

"May I ask whose visage you carry inside?"

Her cheeks turned pink, and his heart seemed to stop as suddenly the pieces of the puzzle began to fit themselves together. She must love another. That was why she hadn't wanted to meet him, to marry him, why she pushed him away. She was—

"My mother's."

He let out a sigh of relief at the error in his assumption.

"Have you always worn it?" he asked.

"Since I left home," she said. "We are close. Closer than most mothers and daughters, I would say."

"I suppose that may be because you have no other siblings," he said, trying to do all he could to learn more about her.

"I am all she has," she said, biting her lip.

"Well, your father is with her," he said helpfully and was shocked at the dark look that passed over Scarlett's face.

"That just makes things worse," she muttered.

"Pardon me?" he asked, wondering if he had heard her correctly.

"Nothing."

"Your parents are not agreeable with one another?" They wouldn't be the only couple of the *ton* to not be amiable, that was for certain. Yet he hadn't sensed any ill will at the wedding.

"They get along fine," she said, her posture stiff. "As my father also does with his mistress and other ladies, while my mother waits at home for him — the man she loves — to return to her."

Hunter was speechless, and Scarlett brought a hand to her hair, beginning to worry a strand that framed her face in response to his astonishment. He closed his jaw.

"I shouldn't have said that." Her words came out in a rush. "Forget I mentioned anything about it. My apologies. I've ruined dinner, and it hasn't even started. My parents are fine."

He sat there staring at her, as suddenly it all began to make sense. Why she held him at arm's length, why she hadn't wanted to marry. She didn't want to end up like her mother. She was like a wounded dog, lashing out to protect herself before another could hurt her even worse.

"Scarlett, I—"

"I said I do not want to discuss it." She picked up her wine and took a long swallow.

"Very well," he said softly. "It must be difficult to be away from your mother now."

Scarlett's lashes fell, hiding her eyes.

"It is," she said. "I do visit, though, as she is less than a half day's ride away."

"Do you plan on seeing her soon?"

"I had thought to leave for a visit when you depart for London."

"Ah," he said, and the conversation died between them. Finally, he added, "I expect I will leave tomorrow after I visit some of my tenants and meet with Stone."

"Oh!" she exclaimed, her eyes flying up to meet his at his words. "You have decided to look further into what I have told you of, then?"

"I have looked at the general ledgers," he said cautiously. "I must do more investigating before I can accuse Stone of anything. I really don't think there is any cause for concern, though, Scarlett. The man has been with my family for years."

"Then his word is worth more than your wife's?"

He took a deep breath as he tried to keep his patience.

"I am going to visit them, tomorrow, Scarlett, does that mean nothing to you?"

She shrugged. "It is something, I suppose. They will be pleased to see you, I am sure."

Hunter hadn't realized his butler, Abbot, had entered the room, but he started when he heard him speak behind him.

"I am sure they would like to see the two of you together," he said, and Hunter turned to him in surprise. The butler didn't make eye contact with him but also didn't seem embarrassed at speaking so out of turn.

"Perhaps they would," he murmured as he turned back to his venison.

And now that he finally knew the reasoning behind Scarlett's reluctance to draw closer to him, he was going to do all he could to break through the wall she had built around herself, and find a way through. The problem was, he only had a day to do it, for much more urgent matters awaited him.

Scarlett fidgeted with the stem of her wine glass. Why had she told Hunter of her parents? She hadn't intended to share anything with him, but then it had just slipped out. *Fool*, she cursed. Now he wore that self-satisfied grin as though he had figured out everything about her. It was but one piece of information. In reality, he knew nothing.

She desperately searched for a way to change the subject, suddenly remembering Marion's request.

"I have a rather odd question for you," she said, bringing the drink to her lips.

"Yes?" Hunter asked, raising his head, and when his eyes met hers with such intensity, shock coursed through her, sending shivers down her spine, all the way up to her suddenly quivering center. She blinked rapidly as she struggled to release herself from his spell.

"Ah, yes," she said. "It's about your valet."

"Spicer?" An eyebrow arched quizzically.

"Yes," she said, forging on. "Is he attached to anyone?"

"Besides me?" Hunter asked with a laugh.

"A woman," she said sardonically.

"Why?" he asked, leaning back in his chair. "Are you interested?"

"No!" she exclaimed, but seeing his teasing grin, she relaxed. "My lady's maid, Marion. She had ... questions about him."

"How very *friendly* of you," he said, a curious expression crossing his face, and she tilted her nose up into the air.

"Do you take exception with the fact that I see to the affairs of my lady's maid?"

He shrugged. "Not at all. Most ladies wouldn't take the time to speak of such things with a servant, lady's maid or not."

"I am not most ladies."

"That, Scarlett, I am beginning to understand."

She eyed him then, taking in the small smirk that teased the corner of his lips, and she wasn't sure whether she should be complimented or insulted. She chose to let the matter rest and said nothing, but simply waited for him to answer her.

"Spicer is unattached, as far as I am aware," he finally said. "Whether he has interest in your maid, I have no idea. I don't suppose you would like me to look into this matter?"

"Would you?" she asked hopefully. She didn't want to be indebted to him for anything, but Marion had done enough for her that she owed her this at least.

Hunter sighed. "Fine," he said, waving a hand in the air. "I will speak to Spicer, but that is where my part in this matchmaking business ends."

"Wonderful," she beamed at him. The fact that he was willing to see to the affairs of his servants was promising, for then perhaps he would begin to open up to changes with his tenants as well. Tomorrow would be interesting, she mused. She hoped his eyes would be opened to all that he had been blind to, as he was always so focused on his affairs in London.

"Tell me, *Hunter*," she said, seeing the surprise on his face, and she smiled inwardly that she had achieved her purpose. "What do you enjoy so much about attending the House of Lords? I know many a man who is not nearly so regular as you are. Yet it is more important to you than all else."

He was silent for a moment, as he seemed to be contemplating her question, and likely considering what she might be insinuating regarding his attention to their marriage.

"All who are part of the House of Lords have been born into the role," he said, his blue-green eyes beginning to gleam. "It is a privilege, and yet many see it as a burden. I do know, Scarlett, that perhaps I should be a slightly better landlord, get to know the people, and all that. But we have the ability to create change, to make all of Great Britain a better place. Yes, some issues that come up may seem so small as to not be worthy of our time, but the truth is, what may seem like a tiny matter makes a consequential difference to someone, somewhere."

"I cannot say I have seen much change in the past number of years."

"No." He shook his head and rolled his glass between his fingers. "This may be true. But I hope that will not be the case for much longer. There are ... places, Scarlett, that you cannot even imagine. Where children work harder than a grown man should. Where prisoners or the insane are treated worse than pigs. And why? Simply because someone has been given the authority to treat them so? These people must be protected. And who else can do so if not us?"

Scarlett stared at him in shock. He was not the man she had thought he was, not the man she had assumed him to be. She had thought he simply enjoyed his role in the House because it was a sort of prestige above most others. But he actually appreciated his capacity to do something with his position.

"You are wrong," she finally said.

"What?"

"I have seen some of these places myself." She leaned forward on the table toward him though sat back hastily when she saw Hunter's eyes dip near level with the table and she suddenly recalled her rather low neckline. She cleared her throat. "You are right, Hunter. We are born to play a role. And I believe a part of that role is to help others who are less well off than we are. I have been to hospitals, to orphanages, and visited with the men, women, and children, have seen what they needed, have provided what I can. And I think that what you are doing is admirable."

He blinked, clearly as shocked by her words as she had been by his.

"So what you are doing with my tenants — that is an extension of charity work you have done before?"

"I suppose." She shrugged. "It is a start, anyway, though I should like to do more."

He nodded. "Scarlett. We seem to have similar goals, similar ideals. What do you say we stop working against one another and try to do this together?"

She stilled, her fork halfway to her mouth. Did he mean it? It was more than she would have expected a man to allow for his wife. She paused. Was there a reason for his offer? In her experience, when a man gave a woman something she desperately wanted, it was only because there was something he needed from her in turn.

"I would say," she said with some hesitation, "we could discuss it."

"Very well, then!" he said, a smile breaking across his face, lighting his handsome features, and it seemed as though her heart flipped over in her chest. "Tomorrow, after our visit? Before I return to London?"

"Ah, yes," she said, disappointment crashing over her. One cordial conversation and she completely forgot the nature of their relationship and their two distinct lives, separate from one another. She well knew that the House didn't sit again until March. Was he really that eager to get away from her once more? She should take this opportunity, however, to take hold of what he offered her. "Tomorrow."

What would the day hold?

7

Hunter knew better now than to look for his wife in the house. Sure enough, after he trampled through the fresh snow that had fallen overnight and entered the stable, there she was, making her rounds from one horse to the next. The woman loved the animals, that was for certain. He didn't recognize the mount she had ridden the other day, and he assumed she had brought the horse with her.

"Of course," she said when he asked that very question as he strode into the barn, causing her to whirl around at his voice and the sound of his footsteps through the straw. "I could never leave Star behind. Why, he would have no way to understand what was happening or why we were being separated. We have also been together long enough that no other horse knows me as he does."

"He's a fine horse," he agreed, coming to stand next to her, as he stroked the horse's mane, his hand less than an inch from Scarlett's, their shoulders brushing. He could feel her stiffen beside him, and she stepped back, but not before her scent washed over him. She smelled like ... spruce trees, he thought, and something akin to frankincense. For all he knew, it could have been some kind of love potion, for the way that it captivated him, pulling him toward her.

"...take the sleigh?"

Hunter shook his head, realizing that he had been so focused on watching her walk away from him, her hips swaying back and forth beneath her riding habit, that he hadn't listened to anything she was saying.

"I asked if you would want to take the sleigh out this morning."

"The sleigh?" What was she on about? "Why in heaven's name would we want to take the sleigh? It's old and it's cumbersome, and it will take us much longer to travel from one place to the next."

"Not today," she said, turning to him with a raised eyebrow. "Did you not just walk across the same yard that I did? It's covered in a foot of snow! The wheels of the carriage are likely to become stuck and then you will never find your way back to London. We cannot simply ride the horses as I have items to take with me. Besides," she said, chewing her lip and a wistful look came over her eye. It was then he knew that she had him. How could he say no to a face like hers, the one time she asked something of him? "It's near Christmas, and a sleigh ride is always fun this time of year."

It was his turn to bristle. She had shown him not an ounce of warmth, but suddenly she was the type of woman who became nostalgic over Christmastide celebrations? "Christmas is but another day on the calendar, Scarlett," he said, shaking his head. "There is nothing significant about the day, besides the fact it is a religious holiday, and all the sleigh rides and dinners won't change that."

He had said it nonchalantly, but when he looked over at

her, he was shocked by the incredulous expression she wore on her face. Her hands were on her hips, her eyes wide and her lips parted slightly.

"What?" he asked, running a hand through his hair, which he never allowed Spicer to wet on his head, despite the current style. He didn't have time to worry about vanities like that. "Did I say something to offend you?"

"That's ... so sad," she said, her voice just above a whisper. "How could you not care for Christmas?"

Pieces of dust and straw circled her head in the light that entered through slats in the wood of the stable, highlighting the beautiful planes of her face, and she looked so crushed that he felt guilty for a moment — which was ridiculous.

"It's just never been important," he said, brushing by her, not wanting to discuss it any further, and seeing her staring at him so, those hazel eyes boring into him, made him want to tell her anything she wanted to know.

"Well," she said following him as he went to find the groom. "It is to me."

"Nia always wanted to celebrate Christmas," he muttered. "No one ever found the time."

"What was that?" she came up beside him so quickly that her deep purple riding skirts whirled around her, and he caught himself before he revealed anymore.

"Nothing," he said. "Nothing at all. Ah, Carver, there you are!" Relief filled him as the groom came into sight. "Prepare..." He looked over at Scarlett, who stared at him with a look of such hope that he gave in with a sigh. "The sleigh," he said. "Prepare the sleigh."

As much as he hated to admit it, Scarlett had been right.

The sleigh *was* the best conveyance to cut through his land. He hadn't seen her fill the sleigh with anything, but with a quick look at the full bags within it and then a glance over at Scarlett and the satisfaction on her face, told him that this had been her plan from the beginning.

"This was nice of Carver, providing us with a blanket and a warming stone," she said, though a bit of consternation entered her tone. "He only sent one though. I suppose we will have to share."

"It's fine, I'm not cold. Carver's normally not quite so shortsighted," he murmured. "I'll speak with him when we return."

"Don't," she said, placing a gloved hand over his, and when his gaze flew up to hers, she hastily pulled it away. "He's a nice boy, truly, and I don't want any trouble. I'm sure he just forgot. We were rather hasty."

"I suppose," he said, looking into the distance, seeing the smoke rising from a chimney. "Here's Thomas and Molly Baker's house."

"I know," she said, and he looked over at her, remembering Stone's information regarding the money she gave to the families. How often had she been out here?

He pulled on the reins when they reached the drive, and when he turned to help Scarlett out of the sleigh, he was surprised to see that she was already on the ground and making her way down the cleared path in her sturdy black boots. "Bring a basket!" she called to him as she rounded the stone entrance, and just then a little figure came hurtling out the door to greet her.

"Lady Oxford!" the boy cried as he barreled into her while Hunter watched with astonishment. Never in his life had he seen such a sight before. His mother would be utterly horrified if she knew Scarlett was even speaking with the families let alone — was she lifting the boy in the air?

"Fly, birdie!" she cried, and the boy erupted in giggles as she spun him in a circle. He couldn't have been more than four, he thought, as he watched from the sleigh, finally lifting the cover to reveal a pile of baskets, full of candies and liquor bottles and heaven only knew what else Scarlett had placed inside them. Good Lord, how much had this cost him?

"Bobby, let Lady Oxford come in — it's freezing out there!" called a laughing voice from the doorway. "Lady Oxford, how lovely to see you!"

"How many times must I tell you, Molly, that Scarlett is just fine?" she said, a grin coming over her face as she made her way around the fenced pig enclosure to the entrance of the small cabin.

Scarlett? The woman who insisted on calling her husband Lord Oxford was telling a common woman to call her Scarlett? Hunter certainly didn't look down on these people the way many of his class did, but he had never in his life expected Scarlett to hold them in such high esteem. Where was the cold woman he had come to know, who ate dinner in near silence, who hardly spoke to him with the exception of polite conversation when required?

Stunned, he began to follow her up the path, and just when Molly Baker was about to shut the door, she caught sight of him.

"Oh, my lord," she said, lifting her worn brown skirt as she sank into a curtsy. "My apologies, my lord, I didn't see you there. We were not aware you were in residence, and therefore were not expecting you. Not that you require any advance notice. That is — oh dear, I am rambling on. Please, do come in."

She opened the door wider, and the warmth of the fire in the corner of the small room drew him in. He might have declined to share the blanket, but he had to admit that the chill in the air was beginning to seep into his bones.

"Thank you, Mrs. Baker," he said with a nod. "My arrival was unexpected, I will admit, but I am pleased to have the opportunity to visit with you."

"Of course," she said, turning her head sharply when she heard voices behind her rise in argument. "Children!" she hissed. "Our lord is here to visit. Come say hello."

Four young ones of various heights dutifully dropped the doll they were fighting over and lined up in front of him, while the boy he had first seen stood beside Scarlett, his fist wrapped around the material of her skirt. The door at the back of the house opened and Thomas Baker walked in, stomping his boots at the entrance to rid them of snow.

"Gads, it's a frosty one out there, I tell ya, Molly. It—"

"We have visitors, Tom."

"My lord! Welcome," he said with a nod, but when his head turned to Scarlett, ruddy coloring infused his cheeks, which had certainly not been present when his attention had been directed toward Hunter.

"Lady Oxford," he said, "How lovely to see you. Bobby's already latched himself to you, has he?"

"He certainly has," she said with a laugh. "How are you, Thomas?"

"Just fine," he said. "Though I've had to bring the animals into the shelter, as cold as it's gotten out there. It seems this snow isn't letting up. Are you sure you should be out in this weather?"

"We'll be fine," she said with a smile. "We aren't far from the house."

Hunter felt as though he were watching a boxing match

as his head swung back and forth between them, conversing as though *she* were the landowner and not him. He should be the one speaking about such with his tenant.

"Thomas," he said, feeling like an interloper as he cut into their conversation. "Have you a moment to discuss a few matters?"

"Of course, my lord," he responded.

"Here, allow me to prepare you some tea," said Molly, as she began bustling around the room, shooing the children out of the kitchen. Hunter looked over at Scarlett, inclining his head toward Molly, suggesting that perhaps she speak with the woman while he discussed matters with her husband, but Scarlett looked away, pretending that she misunderstood his cue, although Hunter knew she was much smarter than that. He sighed. She was a handful, this one.

"Thomas," he began, taking a seat in a scarred wooden chair which matched the table in front of it. "It has been some time since I have been here myself, as I have left my matters of estate business in the capable hands of Mr. Stone."

Scarlett snorted from her seat beside him, and he cast a look of disapproval her way. They had to be united in front of their tenants, not questioning one another. He looked back at Thomas, who had covered his mouth with his hand, and Hunter had the distinct impression the man was hiding a smile.

"How fares your work?" he asked, pretending Scarlett wasn't there beside him. "Have you had any particular issues?"

Thomas cleared his throat, glancing at both Molly and Scarlett in turn, before returning his gaze to Hunter. Scarlett sent a nod the man's way, and Hunter's irritation rose anew.

"I cannot say we've had an easy time of it lately, my lord," he said with a bit of hesitation, and Hunter smiled, encouraging him to continue. "You see ... the rent is just too high for us to make a go of it. Try as I might, I don't make enough off sale of the animals to cover the payments as well as feed and clothe my children. If it wasn't for Lady Oxford ... well, I'm not sure that we would be able to continue on here, my lord. She has been generous, but I would feel much better knowing I had less to pay up front. I know that is much to ask, and I shouldn't like to be presumptuous, but, well, I'm not sure what else to say."

Thomas dropped his head, and Hunter realized how much it had cost him to humble himself as he had in front of him.

"I see," he said grimly. "Thank you for your honesty, Thomas. I will be looking into the matter, I can assure you."

He spoke with the man for a few minutes more about various aspects of pig farming, though Hunter knew far less of it than he cared to admit. Eventually, he stood and shook the man's hand.

"Thank you for your visit," Thomas said, and finally the warmth he had bestowed upon Scarlett came over his face as he looked at Hunter.

"And before we forget," said Scarlett, finally breaking into the conversation, "We have something for you." She took the basket that Hunter had set it by the door. "Happy Christmas," she enthused. "We will see you soon!"

The young boy gave her one last hug before they were on their way, back to the sleigh, Scarlett waving goodbye as the family watched from the door. When she turned to face forward, a guarded expression settled over her face, and all Hunter could do was wonder — who was this woman he had married?

8

The longer they sat there in silence, the more anxious Scarlett became. What was going through his head? Her husband had entered the sleigh, taken the reins in hand, and then sat there immobile, his gaze off into the distance. Was he angry with her? Not that he had any reason to be, she told herself. She was simply allowing him to see the truth.

"It seems you were right," he said, his voice breaking through the whisper of the slight wind that had begun to brew, his breath casting smoke into the cold air. "I have been a terribly remiss lord."

He paused for a moment, opening his mouth a couple of times until he finally continued speaking. "If I had asked Thomas how much rent is, he would have realized this as well, and yet I must know before I meet with Stone. How much are their rents?"

When she told him, he whistled. It was more than double what he would have expected. No wonder his tenants were having difficulties.

"How did I let this happen?" he asked, hanging his head

somewhat, and Scarlett felt inexplicable sympathy come over her.

Stop it, this is his own doing. And isn't this what you wanted — for him to see the error of his ways? He should have paid much more attention. But the look of remorse covering his face spoke to the fact that he had placed his absolute trust in the wrong person, and she could not keep her heart from going out to him.

"Sometimes the people we think we can rely on the most end up causing us the greatest distress," she said, and he looked up at her with disappointment etched in his blue-green eyes — disappointment in himself.

"I have become caught up in my work in London," he said, looking back out into the snow-covered distance. "In doing so, I have forgotten my responsibility here. But it is more than work. My decisions affect every aspect of these people's lives. No wonder you think so poorly of me."

She bit her lip. He was right, in a way, but what he didn't know was that it wasn't that she disdained of him so. No, there were aspects about him that she actually admired — his dedication, his ability to keep from becoming so inflexible that he couldn't see the error in his ways. He was simply absent-minded about aspects of his life that he needed to pay more attention to. Perhaps it was a failing, but not one that was born of any necessary evil or ill intention.

No, what kept her from him was the fact that she could see herself becoming *too* close to him, and that would never do. For she knew what she spoke of when she told him that people could be a disappointment. Her own father had been so time and again. He loved her, she knew, but that hadn't been enough. While he provided for her and was there when she asked him for anything, as a true father, he hadn't been there for her when she needed him, nor there for her mother at any time at all.

As much as she had to protect herself, however, she should be more conscious of not allowing Hunter to feel too poorly for himself.

"This is nothing that you cannot fix," she said gently, leaning forward so that she could look into his eyes. "You have the power to change this, to make things better here. Besides that," she couldn't help the grin from crossing her face. "I was here to make things right."

He looked at her then, his face but inches from hers, and her heart began to quicken, beating fast enough for her blood to begin to race through her body, warming all which had become so cold in the freezing air.

"Hunter," she said, her voice a whisper. "Hunter, I—"

The horse whinnied then, breaking the moment, and she sat back suddenly. "I think we best get a move on," she said, clearing her throat, "we must see to the other tenants. Do you know what time it is?"

He shook his head, saying nothing as he sent the horses on their way.

"Do you not have a pocket watch?"

"No," he said shortly, surprising her.

"You don't have a pocket watch?" she looked at him, perplexed. "Every man has a pocket watch."

"I don't."

"Why not?"

"No one ever gave me one."

"Could you not have bought your own?"

He shrugged. "I suppose I could have. But ... it simply didn't seem right."

Sensing his reluctance to speak on the topic, she

frowned in consternation but didn't question him any further.

SHE HAD NEARLY KISSED HIM. Twice now, he had been close to taking her lips with his, and twice she had pulled away. What kind of man was he, that he couldn't even convince his own wife to kiss him? Not only that, he had nearly broken down, had nearly told her of his own disappointment. He had asked his father for a pocket watch just like his, but his father always told him to earn enough money to buy his own.

Well, Hunter thought, he would have to forget that for the moment, for he had a role to play — the role of the focused landlord. They visited one house after another, bearing baskets and a promise of lower rents in the new year. Hunter was overcome with the joy on the faces of his tenants. What truly took him aback, however, was their reaction to Scarlett. They all loved his wife, welcoming her into their homes as though she were an old friend instead of the new wife of their lord. How often had she visited? He had never seen anything like it in all his years.

He finally asked her about it as he turned the sleigh back toward Wintervale.

"Why am I so friendly with them?" she asked, fixing her gaze upon him. "Because they are people, Hunter. People who I enjoy speaking with. For the past three months, I have been alone with them — and the servants of course, and then there is Lavinia, but she is not always around — and I enjoy their company. Besides, it is important to ensure they are happy. It is better for you at the end of the day."

He nodded, wondering as he did if *she* was happy alone

here on his estate. As though she heard his thoughts, however, she continued.

"I love it out here," she said wistfully. "It is so open, so free, and you have a beautiful home, Hunter, truly you do. I couldn't imagine being stuck in London for months on end, as you are. I actually feel sorry for you, that you must be."

He certainly didn't feel sorry for himself. He loved his work there — though he understood what she said regarding the freedom of the country and he wished once more he spent more time here.

"Oh, look!" she said, pointing to a path just visible through the evergreens. "This is where I wanted to stop."

"Stop for what?" he asked.

"Boughs for the house! You are apparently not the only one who dislikes Christmas, Hunter, for there is not a decoration to be found within all of Wintervale. We looked everywhere, though Abbot and Mrs. Shepherd, as well as Lavinia, assured me I would come up empty. It seems Christmas is not a family tradition. Which is sad, really, as that is what Christmas is all about. I ordered some things, but others we must collect ourselves. Here, stop now."

He slowed the horses, though he wanted nothing more than to continue on toward home. He really did have to be going if he wanted to make it to London. As he thought of it, a snowflake dropped onto the tip of his nose, and he looked around to see a multitude of them falling around them.

"It's snowing again!" she said, a look of glee coming over her face, and he couldn't help but stop now, wanting to see more of this woman who had revealed herself to him today in the homes of his tenants. If Christmas was going to bring some happiness to her, well, he supposed for an hour he could stop and allow her to enjoy it. And then, when they returned to the house, he really had to be on his way, or he would never make it to London in time.

"All right, then," he said, sharing her smile. "What do you need me to do?"

"Come!" she exclaimed with the same enthusiasm Bobby had held earlier. "You can carry for me."

"Carry?"

His question was soon answered, however, as she piled bough after bough in his arms or the bag which had previously held the baskets for the tenants. She picked up all of the pieces of evergreens that had fallen to the ground, before carefully selecting other types of greenery. It all looked the same to Hunter, but she seemed to know exactly what each type of shrub or tree was, adding all to her collection. He dragged the filled bag back to the sleigh, before returning to hold the rest himself. He was relieved when she finally seemed satisfied, for he didn't think he could carry anything else without it all falling to the ground.

"I think that should do, for now at least," she said, bounding back toward the sleigh, while he followed much more slowly, trying to balance everything. "Oh, Wintervale will look so lovely once all of this is strewn about."

"Where do you even plan on putting this?" he asked, his voice muffled as his face was entirely covered by branches.

"Everywhere!" she exclaimed. "There is nothing like the feeling of Christmas, Hunter. It enters your very soul, filling you with a warmth unlike anything else. Have you truly never felt it?"

He finally relieved himself of his burden, dropping it into the sleigh, before turning back toward her. He seemed to forget how to breathe entirely, however, when he looked at her face. Those eyes which had regarded him with so much chagrin were now glistening with exhilaration, her cheeks were rosy as could be from the cold air, and her lips red and inviting. Finally, her walls had come down, and he was not going to let this moment pass.

"I suppose," he said slowly and carefully, drawing closer to her. "I am beginning to feel it now."

He leaned down then, determined that this time, she would not escape. He saw a tiny bit of panic flare in her eyes as his face neared hers, but she didn't back away. He brought his hand to the back of her head, and before she could have another moment to think about what was happening between them, he brought his lips to hers.

It had taken months, but he finally tasted his wife. And now that he had sampled, he wanted more. He didn't want to scare her away, but it was difficult to keep himself from taking more than this sweet, chaste kiss. He could sense her hesitancy, however, so he held himself to what she offered, her lips soft and warm under his. So as not to scare her, he began to slowly move them over hers, tempting, slightly teasing, and he knew the moment she allowed her resistance to begin to ebb away. For her body, so tense and tight, began to sink into him seemingly of its own will, the ice beginning to melt as her soft form came flush against his. He ran his tongue over the seam of her lips, and she opened to him, allowing him in, and he felt the exhilaration down to his very soul.

For he knew this was more than simply sharing a kiss with her husband. This was opening up to him in more than just the physical sense.

She tasted like the spice of the pastry she had been offered at their last stop, and, like the temptation of sugar, he wanted more of her — more than was appropriate to ask here, in the middle of these evergreens, the snow beginning to swirl around them. In fact, when he finally broke away, he was shocked to find the snow was now coming down in droves. When had that happened?

He looked down to find her staring up at him in amazement, and he was filled with a sense of satisfaction that it took a moment for her to come back to her senses.

"I — Hunter, I—"

He shook his head, smiling at her. "You don't have to say anything," he murmured, stroking her red cheek with his gloved thumb. "But we should get back."

She looked around her, taking in the sudden snowfall with as much surprise as he had.

"Goodness, but it's coming down!" she exclaimed. "We should go."

This time, when they took a seat in the sleigh, he lifted the blanket over both of them, feeling her leg pressed against his. When she didn't move away, he smiled. Perhaps there was something to the Christmas spirit after all.

9

————

"Oh, my lord, my lady!" Mrs. Shepherd hurried toward the door as they let themselves in, shaking off the snow. Scarlett looked over at Hunter and couldn't help but begin to laugh, for the snow covered his riot of curls as though he were wearing a powdered wig. It was quickly beginning to melt as they stood in the entrance of the foyer, plastering the curls to his forehead. She was compelled to reach out and brush them away from his face, but stilled her hand before it acted of its own accord.

"My, but it's frightfully cold out there!" Mrs. Shepherd continued, bustling around them as she helped Scarlett with her cloak. "You're both going to catch a death of a cold if you don't warm yourselves at once. My lord, where is your hat? Come, come."

Scarlett smiled warmly at the woman who reminded her of a nursemaid the way she was fretting over the two of them. It was sweet, though, really, and she allowed her to continue her ministrations.

Abbot walked into the room then, his march the same

steady pace he continued wherever he went. The house could be on fire and Abbot would still move with his measured steps out the door.

"My lord," he said, "Spicer has prepared everything for your departure, but he wonders whether you might prefer to stay the night, with the way the weather has turned."

Scarlett looked over at Hunter, who cocked his head to the side as he contemplated Abbot's words. He turned toward the door as though he could see through it and he sighed.

"Perhaps you are right, Abbot. It has grown rather late, and it will be difficult to see through the snow. I am to have dinner tomorrow with Lord Falconer, but if I leave in the morning we should still be able to make it in time. I have items of importance I wanted to discuss before he departs for his own country home, so that everything will be in order by the time Session resumes. However, if I ready my notes tonight, then I shouldn't need to do so once I make London. Yes, that will be well."

Was he speaking to her, to Abbot, or to himself? He had begun wandering through the adjoining Oak Hall as he muttered away, apparently not noticing he was dripping melting snow over the floorboards.

"He'll be going to his study," said Abbot — was that disapproval in his tone as he watched his employer meander down the hall?

Scarlett shook her head as she gathered her skirts and followed after her husband, as her rooms were in the same corridor as the study. Where was the man who had just kissed her in the snow, who had turned the cold into magic swirling around her? He was gone, lost to the Hunter who was completely wrapped up in his work. Though she now knew that his purpose was the admirable sort, she would have preferred that he include her in the conversation, if what he had to see to was so pressing.

This was the problem with men, she thought as the hope that had stirred in her belly simmered into anger. They made you believe one thing, charged your emotions, and then in the next moment they brushed you aside as though it all meant nothing. She rubbed her forehead. She should know better. Well, it was just a kiss. A bit of fun, really.

But as she closed her door and sank back against it, she knew, deep down in her soul, that she was already beginning to lose the battle of defending her own heart.

SCARLETT AWOKE the next day determined to change her focus. She had accomplished her goal with Hunter — she had made him see the error in his ways, demonstrated all that he had been blind to in trusting his steward with sole responsibility of his estate. With any luck, he would be rid of Stone and conditions could begin to turn around for his tenants. It would be a new beginning in the new year.

And *that* was all she needed of him. Nothing more — or so she continued to tell herself.

"Good morning, my lady."

"Good morning, Marion," Scarlett smiled at her maid as she bustled into the room and began to efficiently pull various dresses from the wardrobe.

"What activities have you planned for this morning, my lady?" she asked as she held up a riding habit in one hand and a morning gown in the other.

Scarlett, sitting up under the blankets with her legs crossed, looked up at Marion, sighing as she placed her elbows on her legs and her chin in the palms of her hands, contemplating the girl and the clothing she held.

"I'm not entirely sure," Scarlett said, tilting her head to the side. "I had thought perhaps to return home to visit my mother today for Christmas Eve and Christmas dinner. But first, I did want to add some festivity to this house. I'll be back before Twelfth Night, so will have plenty of time to enjoy it. Besides that, I think the rest of the servants would like it — do you agree?"

"I do, my lady," Marion replied with a convincing nod. "Everyone loves a bit of Christmas, and it doesn't seem this house has ever had any."

"Why do you think that is?"

Marion shrugged. "Mrs. Shepherd said that the family has hardly ever been in residence, as the marquess and marchioness have another home they prefer, and when Lord Oxford has been here, he doesn't celebrate the season at all. Mrs. Shepherd thinks that they have never celebrated Christmas before." Her voice dropped to a whisper, though no one else was near to hear them. "It's rather sad, isn't it my lady?"

"It is," Scarlett agreed. "Well, then, Marion, it is up to us to share it with them. I'll wear the morning dress while we ready this house following breakfast, and then we'll leave this afternoon for my mother's, how does that sound?"

Marion replaced the riding habit but turned around hurriedly. "Oh, my lady! I was so caught up in discussing the decorations that I completely forgot to tell you — while a ride may be possible, there is no way we can make the visit to your mother's today."

"What do you mean?" Scarlett looked at her quizzically.

"The snow, my lady — it came down all night!"

Scarlett pushed back the blankets, shivering as her feet

touched the wooden floor. This room needed a carpet near the bed. It was an unusually cold winter, that was for certain. She padded over to the window, gasping when she looked out below. For what had been a foot of snow the day before had turned into mountains of it overnight. The snow blanketed everything — the maple trees, which were bare with the winter, the evergreens, and all of the gardens that stretched out below her south-facing window.

"My goodness!" she exclaimed. "I'll never make it through there, even on horseback." She whirled around to look at Marion. "And Lord Oxford will certainly not be able to London."

Marion shook her head, the slightest of smiles curling the edges of her lips. Ah, yes — the valet. It meant he would be staying as well. "No, my lady," she said. "It seems you will be spending Christmas with the earl."

"MRS. SHEPHERD!" Scarlett called into the maid's sitting room as she looked for the housekeeper, Marion trailing behind her. Mrs. Shepherd came bustling out of the room, Abbot following along behind her.

"Ah, there you are!" Scarlett exclaimed. "Splendid. Now, Lord Oxford and I collected greenery yesterday while we were visiting the tenants, and it must still be in the sleigh. I'd like to decorate the house this morning, being that it is already Christmas Eve, and that will be decidedly important. Oh! And my mother wrote and said she would be sending mistletoe, which one of her friends brought up from the south. Did it arrive?"

"It did, my lady, earlier this week, and we will be

readying it. Not to worry, we will have the house prepared for you by tomorrow."

"Oh, but Mrs. Shepherd, I would love nothing more than to help. Is there any ribbon about? Or paper, perhaps? Come, let's arrange everything in the blue drawing room."

It was small, private, and Scarlett had taken it on as her own private sitting room. It had been rather cold when she first arrived, but now it was filled with her favorite things that she had brought with her from her parents' home — the quilt her nursemaid had knitted for her, the small paintings and portraits of family members that reminded her of home.

Now, the footmen were lining greenery upon the floor, and Scarlett took command, instructing the maids on how to create the perfect boughs and balls of greenery.

"And this," she said with flourish as she picked up a piece of it, "is mistletoe. Careful now, young ladies, that you don't find yourself below it with a man who may not be of your choosing." She winked at Marion, who blushed up to the roots of her auburn hair. Scarlett had noticed the valet, Spicer, had paid particular attention to Marion this morning. When Scarlett asked him where his lord was, he said she could find him in his study. Scarlett simply shrugged, deciding that it didn't matter.

"Marion," she murmured to her maid in a low voice, drawing her over to the side of the room, next to the marble fireplace, where a cheery fire burned. "I completely forgot to tell you. It seems your Mr. Spicer *is* unattached. And now, you shall spend Christmas with him. I do hope all works out well for the two of you, but promise me you will be careful?"

Marion simply smiled and turned away, and Scarlett pulled at a strand of hair that had fallen out of her messy chignon, winding it around her finger as she contemplated

ELLIE ST. CLAIR

Marion and Spicer, who were now shyly conversing. Perhaps love *could* work for some, she thought wistfully as she tied together the ball of mistletoe along with some of the evergreen boughs they had picked from the forest floor. She pushed back the memories of yesterday that continued to try to invade. *It meant nothing. Simply a bit of fun.*

Scarlett gathered a large bundle of greenery as she made her way through the sitting room, passing through the Green Room, where she smiled at some of the footmen. It seemed the servants were rather enjoying this bit of festivity, as everywhere she looked all were getting in on the fun. Oak Hall — *that* was where she would focus her attention. It branched off the foyer and was continually used to reach nearly every other room of the house, by both herself and the servants alike.

Determining the best placement for her boughs, she began to retrace her steps, nearly running into the valet.

"Ah, Spicer," she said with a smile, and he returned her look with a youthful grin. "Do you suppose you could fetch the library steps? I was thinking to hang this from the entrance into the room."

"Of course, my lady," he said, and returned moments later with the wooden steps, which reached fairly high, perfect for the tall bookshelves that lined the library. "Allow me."

"No, no, I am perfectly fine," she said, then remembering Marion tying together the greenery in the drawing room, she was inspired. "I am sorry to ask another favor of you, but I don't suppose you could fetch me more boughs?"

"Of course, my lady," he said. "I'll be back shortly."

"Take your time," she said sweetly, then began the climb up the steps.

Standing on the top step, she estimated she was still

about an inch from the frame of the doorway, despite standing on the very tips of her toes and reaching as far as she was able. She only needed to stand on the very top of the steps, flush with the railing, and then she could reach the doorframe. She had always had decent balance, likely from years atop a horse. She took a step, smiling when she was at the correct height.

"Here we are," she murmured, fastening the ribbon to the top. "Perf—" Her words were cut off with a shout, however, as the ladder began teetering beneath her. She flailed her arms wildly as she attempted to regain her balance, but suddenly there was nothing to which she could affix her foot, as the steps began to tip forward. She cringed as she prepared herself to meet the floor, but instead of hardwood crashing into her back, she was caught by a pair of arms that seemed to come out of nowhere. She opened her eyes to find her husband's handsome face before her.

Hunter's arms tightened around her, and she could feel his warmth through her dress. He pulled her even closer, as though he could keep her safer that way. "My God, you scared me." His forehead came to hers, his lips but a breath away. Her pulse quickened, in part from her near-fall, but also from *him*. Oh, she could tell herself he had no effect on her, but her body was saying something entirely different.

When his lips descended, she met them with a desperation she didn't know was inside of her. What was she doing? This was *not* following in line with her intentions. All thought left her, however, as he drank her in, and she felt as though she were drowning, from his taste to his touch to the weightless feeling from simply being held by him.

His lips left hers just as abruptly as he had kissed her, but he continued to hold her, the two of them staring at one another, his breathing just as ragged as hers.

Get ahold of yourself, Scarlett. Her attachment to him was growing, but as soon as the weather broke and the roads cleared, he would be back in London and she would be left here, alone. As the thoughts flooded in, she dropped her head, breaking their connection. When she looked back up, Hunter's eyebrows had come together in a vee as he looked at her with some consternation.

"What were you doing?" he asked, his voice a mix of incredulity as well as a thread of anger.

"Decorating," she managed. She would *not* be cowed by him, though it was difficult to focus when she was still slightly shaken from her near-fall.

"What were you thinking?" he demanded now as he strode toward one of the chairs lining the side of the room, setting her down upon it as he crouched beside her. "You were standing on the very top of the ladder! You could have killed yourself."

"Well," she replied calmly, her hand fisting around her locket, twisting it from side to side as she felt the need to defend herself. "I didn't, now did I?"

He ran a hand through his curls as he stood and paced before her. "What is going on here, anyway? My entire staff is bustling around, covering the house in ... in trees!"

"Do you not recall last night?" she asked, raising her eyebrows, and when he stopped his movements and looked back at her, she knew he was remembering more than simply gathering some greenery.

"Of course I do," he muttered. "But I never thought this would be the result."

"This is Christmas, Hunter," she said primly, "and as we are both stuck here, you best get used to it."

10

How could she sit there so calmly, as though nothing had just happened? Hunter had thought that his heart would leap out of his chest when he wandered into Oak Hall looking for his valet, and instead discovered his wife teetering dangerously on the top of a ladder. What if he hadn't arrived in time? She could now be stretched out on the floor below him. She could have broken her neck, for goodness sake, and now she sat here, admonishing him for not enjoying the fact that she was littering his house with the scattering of trees and plants from outside.

"You're right about one thing," he muttered. "We are stuck here."

"That's a lovely sentiment regarding spending Christmas with your wife," she said primly, and he looked down at her, at her hands which had finally stopped their fussing and were now folded in the lap of her cream morning dress. He reached down and straightened the material where it had slipped down her shoulder. His fingers stilled when they touched her bare skin, and her eyes dipped toward where they brushed against her. Did she feel the same fire that he did?

His breath caught as she turned her head, her eyes meeting his once more. Why did they captivate him so? He swallowed hard.

"It's only ... it's only that I will be missing an important meeting," he managed. "Of course I am pleased to be here with you."

Her eyes narrowed, and he wasn't sure what he had said that vexed her so, but she didn't seem particularly happy with his response.

"Tell me, Hunter," she said, standing and walking over to the ladder, and he followed her to help her straighten it, her scent of spruce and frankincense strengthened by the boughs around them. The entire house now smelled of her, and it was already driving him mad. "What is it that bothers you so about Christmas? Why did you never celebrate?"

He sighed. He hadn't wanted to speak to her of this, to give her any more of himself until the time she decided to open herself up to him, but it seemed his wife was relentless when she wanted something — just look at the current state of Wintervale.

"My mother hated Christmas," he said, wandering out of the hall into the Green Room beyond, and she followed. He took a seat in front of the fire, to ward off the cold that was filtering in, and she settled herself across from him in a matching Chippendale leather armchair. He shrugged. "There's not much else to say, really. One year Nia decided that she would celebrate Christmas with or without the rest of us. We were here that Christmas. Nia cut boughs off the trees in front of the house — the ones that line the drive, you know which I mean. My father was furious. Said she had ruined the entire aesthetic. She spent the rest of the day crying in her room."

"That's terrible," Scarlett murmured, bowing her head. "What of the other traditions? Do you go to mass? Do you give the servants their Boxing Day gifts?"

"We go to the church service," he said with a shrug. "But only for appearances. There is no special meal after, no Boxing Day, no visit to the tenants as you have already forced upon me. Christmas is just another day."

She cocked her head to the side as she studied him, and despite the frostiness that so often emanated from her, something seemed to melt as she contemplated his words.

"Well, Hunter," she said with conviction. "This year you have no choice but to experience and celebrate Christmas. So you best prepare yourself."

Was that a threat, or a promise?

They both jumped when they heard a slight cough from the doorway of the room, breaking the tension that had filled the air.

"My lady?" It was Spicer, his arms filled with greenery, with Scarlett's lady's maid just visible behind him. Ah, so this was the girl Scarlett had spoken of, who was so interested in his valet. It seemed Spicer wasn't too averse to her attentions, from the way he kept glancing back at her, his cheeks a bright red. "We have the rest of the greenery for this room. Marion — ah, that is, Miss Parker, she has everything well organized for the rest of the house."

Scarlett wore a satisfied grin, and Hunter tried not to chuckle. Somehow, he had a feeling his wife was behind this particular meeting between the pair of them.

"Wonderful!" she said, rising to her feet and clapping her hands together. "Perhaps you can climb the ladder, Spicer, as it seems I'm but an inch too short."

"I'll do it," Hunter heard himself say, and all eyes turned toward him as he stood. For some reason, the thought of another man coming to the aid of his wife stirred a bit of jealousy within him. Which was ridiculous. It was not as though Spicer posed any threat of garnering his wife's affections. But a man needed some pride, now, didn't he?

"You're not ... busy?" Scarlett asked, an eyebrow raised.

"Not anymore," he said with a shrug. "There is no chance of me making my meeting with Lord Falconer tonight, and when I am able to travel, I am already prepared to discuss my proposal."

"You're — you're decorating for Christmas, my lord?" asked Spicer, his eyes wide, and Hunter fixed what he hoped was his best glower on the boy. "Yes, Spicer," he said, trying for patience. "Now, what's next?"

"Here," said Scarlett, picking up the ball of greenery that had fallen from her hand to the floor when Hunter had caught her. "Why don't you hang the mistletoe?"

He raised his eyebrows as he looked at the sprig. "Is that what you nearly killed yourself fixing to the top of the door?"

"I find, Hunter," she said with a saucy grin, "that one can never have too much mistletoe. It provides for a rather fun game of avoiding it — or looking for it — depending on your preference."

She cocked her head at the pair of young servants making eyes at one another near the door, and then winked at Hunter, and he nearly choked. Who was this woman?

SCARLETT HAD to laugh at her husband. As much as he grumbled about the trees she had brought into the house, she could tell he was enjoying himself. Before long, he was getting into the spirit, telling the footmen just where the evergreen boughs should be hung, and arranging the sprigs of ivy, holly, and rosemary over the dining room table with as much precision as a housemaid.

She leaned against the door of the room watching him until he finally must have sensed her presence.

"Are you ready?" she asked him.

"Ready for what?"

"To find the Yule log, of course."

"Can you not just take one of the logs already cut?" he asked, a pained expression on his face, and she couldn't resist teasing him further.

"Of course not," she said. "We must venture into the woods and find the very best."

"Why didn't we simply find one the other day when we were gathering the boughs?"

"Because," she said with an exasperated sigh, "This is a tradition. Every Christmas Eve we choose the Yule Log then light it for the remainder of the season."

"It's Christmas Eve?" he asked with bemusement, and she rolled her eyes at him.

"Of course it is."

"Hmm," he said in wonderment. "I was going to return home today. I didn't realize Lord Falconer would want to meet on Christmas Eve."

"Apparently he has the same regard for the holiday as you do," she said with an arched eyebrow. "Well, I will be going. You are welcome to join or I will meet you here once I have found what I'm looking for. I am rather an expert, you know."

"And what, pray tell, qualifies someone to become an expert at choosing a tree branch?"

"A Yule log," she corrected him with a pointed stare. "It comes from years of experience, Hunter."

"Very well then," he said, feigning disinterest. "I suppose I had better come learn from a master."

She couldn't help the grin that stretched over her face. "I'll meet you outside after I change my gown."

HUNTER HAD THOUGHT they would simply find a tree, cut a log, and be done with it. But no. Scarlett inspected tree after tree, always finding a reason why it didn't suit. Too thin, too thick, too much greenery. Fortunately, they hadn't wandered far from the house, just to the first line of trees in the distance. Wintervale, in fact, was still in sight.

"You know," he remarked, "there are perfectly good logs in the shed beside the manor."

She quelled him into silence with a look, and he threw up his hands. At the very least, the snow had finally stopped falling, though it was piled so high he knew it could be days before he would be able to leave for London. His wife was stuck with him. Although, the frozen walls around her seemed to be melting somewhat, so perhaps now was the time to see if he could bring them down entirely. When she allowed it, she showed him glimpses of the person she was when she wasn't trying desperately to keep as far from him as possible. The woman who gave to his tenants, who was beloved by children and servants alike. Could she find room in her heart for him — and did he want her to? He could admit that the thought scared him a bit, but also brought about a longing that he hadn't known was within him.

"I've found it!" she finally exclaimed, and he breathed a

sigh of relief. He hefted the axe from his shoulder. "Do you have any instructions as to where I should cut?" he asked.

"Here." She drew a line with her finger, and he went to work. It was slow going at first — Hunter hadn't exactly spent his youth outdoors doing hard labor — but soon enough he found a rhythm, and before long his wife's Yule Log lay at her feet.

"Perfect!" she exclaimed, and a thrill ran through him at the joy that overcame her due to something that he had done for her. Well, he supposed, if something so simple could make her happy, then so be it. If only she would look at him the way she looked at the Yule log.

He reached out a hand toward her, though for what purpose he wasn't sure, when a voice cut through the frosty air toward them.

"Hunter? Scarlett? Where in heaven's name are you?"

"Nia!" Scarlett called out, making her way to the break in the trees. "We'll be there momentarily!"

The moment broken, Hunter picked up the log and began trudging after her. Damn his sister. He had been looking forward to another stolen kiss with his wife. It seemed the only way he could capture her was to take her unaware, and he didn't know when he would have another moment like this one. Christmas only lasted so long.

"There you are!" Lavinia called from the doorway. Heaven forbid his sister would spend one moment more than necessary out of doors. "My goodness, I have been looking *everywhere* for you!"

"We can't have been gone more than an hour," Hunter grumbled, and Scarlett shot him a look of consternation.

"It is *lovely* to see you," she emphasized. "How did you make it through the snow?"

"The sleigh, as much as I hate it. But I could hardly

believe it when I heard my brother would be in residence over Christmas! Why, I suppose there is a first for everything. And oh, Scarlett, the house looks absolutely beautiful."

"Doesn't it, though?" Scarlett asked, clasping her hands together.

"I can hardly believe Hunter allowed it!"

"Well," he said, and they both turned to him. "It is not as though I allowed it, exactly. If I had not offered my assistance, I believe Scarlett would have killed herself in an attempt to drape the very ceiling in evergreen boughs."

Lavinia smirked at him, to which he sighed. He loved his sister, but oh, she could be annoying, with her assumptions about his every action.

"You must stay for dinner tonight, Lavinia," Scarlett said. "I know Hunter would love the opportunity to spend time with you. It's been so long."

Actually, Hunter would have preferred to spend the evening better getting to know his wife, but he supposed dinner with Lavinia would have to come first.

At Scarlett's look of encouragement, he forced a smile on his face. "Yes, Nia," he managed. "Do stay for dinner."

"Lovely!" she said, clapping her hands. "I'm so glad you asked because, in fact, I brought Baxter with me. He's waiting in the billiard room. I do believe he has helped himself to your brandy, Hunter, I hope you do not mind. Anyway, you know how I feel about the sleigh and the cold. That is how much I love you, brother. Now, we must discuss tomorrow. We will go to mass and then have a small dinner party, and of course you must attend. Baxter's family was supposed to join us, but with the snow preventing travel, it will likely be the four of us as well as Lord and Lady Raymond — Madeline, of course. We've met them in the village, Scarlett, you remember her? Oh, and I can hardly forget the New Year's party we will have. I told you of that, didn't I? No? Well. It will be great fun, and you must attend."

"Tomorrow is fine. As for New Year's, we — I, ah ... will likely be back in London by then," Hunter managed. He had forgotten that his sister could speak with greater speed and alacrity than even the most experienced lord of the House. And Baxter. He groaned inwardly. The man was an absolute bore. But he loved Lavinia, and for that, Hunter couldn't fault him. "But thank you."

"Well, then, you must come, Scarlett — if you are staying here," she said, to which Scarlett nodded and Hunter's heart fell slightly. He had hoped that perhaps she would change her mind and accompany him back to London. But apparently, a few stolen kisses meant nothing had changed regarding their future together.

"I suppose I should go see to Baxter," he said, handing his cloak to the patiently waiting Spicer.

"My lord," Spicer said in a low voice as he stepped up next to him. "Perhaps before you see to Lord Keppel, you might like to light the Yule log with my lady?"

"Ah, yes, very good, Spicer," he said. If Scarlett took such joy from finding the damn log, then lighting it should be even more thrilling.

"Lady Keppel." Mrs. Shepherd bustled into the room. "How lovely to see you, my dear! I have had Cook prepare your favorite biscuits and they are set out for you in the drawing room. Do come."

Lavinia looked back at Scarlett, clearly torn between seeing the log lit and her waiting biscuits, but Scarlett waved her on. "Go on, Nia," she said. "I'll quickly prepare for dinner and be with you in a moment."

"Very good," his sister said, stealing a glance at Hunter

as well as his wife before smiling surreptitiously and then sauntering out of the room behind the housekeeper.

"Well," said Hunter after a moment when silence stretched between them awkwardly. "We best light the thing, shall we?"

"Yes, let's!" exclaimed Scarlett, clapping her hands together with the excitement of a child, and Hunter grinned. "Where shall we light it, do you think?"

"Oak Hall," he decided immediately. "Then we shall see it every time we walk through."

"That's perfect," she said, smiling at him in approval, and his heart flipped over in his chest. What was this now? Of course he wanted some closeness with his wife, to find some common ground, to try to beget an heir, but he hadn't expected these ... *feelings* to begin to stir for her. It was just the blasted Christmas celebrations. He pushed his emotion aside as he hefted the log in his arms. He would be more than pleased if she overcame her adversity toward him, but he didn't need to become a lovesick pup himself.

They crossed the entrance together and were stepping into Oak Hall when Hunter heard Spicer clear his throat. With some exasperation, he turned to his valet, who stood in the entryway still. What did the man want now?

"Yes, Spicer?" he asked, trying to maintain patience.

"Ah, my lord, it is just that — you are standing under the mistletoe."

"What?"

"The mistletoe," he said in a loud whisper, pointing above Hunter's head at the bough that Scarlett had risked her life to hang. More loudly, he announced, "I shall prepare your evening clothing, my lord."

And with that, Spicer turned and walked the other way, whistling a merry tune.

Hunter turned to his wife to find her staring up at him, a smile teasing her lips. But then she caught his expression and her hazel eyes widened, the gold flecks glinting in the remaining light of day streaming in from the large windows staring down on them.

He threw the Yule log to the floor and took her in his arms, his lips descending on hers. Dear Lord. He was lost.

11

When, upon their marriage, Scarlett had decided to keep her husband as far from her as possible, she hadn't been aware of the fatal flaw within her plan. She had never known the effect his kiss would have upon her.

Every time he kissed her, it seemed as though he was erasing more and more of the lectures her mother had instilled in her, the memories of her father so callously leaving them at any time for all manner of women. Did Hunter feel as she did when their lips met, when their eyes caught and held, or when she walked into a room? The longer she stayed here in this house with him, the more she was drawn to him, and that scared her more than she cared to admit. If only she knew whether she was the only one feeling this way. For this could be how he made many women feel, and before long he would be back in London, leaving her behind as just another part of this estate that he seemed to forget when he wasn't in residence.

When he took her in his arms and his lips came down upon hers hard and unyielding, however, all of these thoughts fled. He kissed her passionately, drinking her up with desperation in the movement of his mouth on hers, his tongue velvet as it caressed her, causing sensations to course through her, sending tingles down her spine. Her body was numb and yet at the same time had never been more alive.

She instinctively pressed herself into him as her arms twined around his neck, her fingers twisting around the locks of curls that she had been yearning to touch for the past few days. He stepped forward with her still in his arms, pressing her against the wall of the entryway, his hands beginning to move now, running up and down her back, her sides, inching up toward her breasts, and she wanted to feel them on her desperately.

"Hunter," she murmured as she tipped her head back from his, but instead of releasing her, he brought his lips to her neck, and she gasped at the sensations caused by his slightest touch. What was this spell he had placed over her?

"Scarlett," he responded, his voice as guttural as she felt. He stepped back, but only to take one of her hands in his. "Come, let's go upst—"

"Ah, there you are, Oxford!"

Scarlett jumped at the intrusion, and Hunter closed his eyes tightly, as though he were willing the man away. He did not, however, release her hand.

"I will be there momentarily, Baxter," he said tightly. "I am busy at the moment."

"Your butler said something about a Yule log. I've always loved a good Yule log, I have. So I said to myself, why am I sitting here enjoying a glass of brandy alone when I could be in front of a roaring fire to welcome the season? So here I am!"

He chuckled, draining the glass in his hand, and Hunter rubbed his forehead with his knuckles. He was murmuring something which Scarlett strained to hear, but when she did, she abruptly stepped back in a bit of shock, though with just as much amusement at his choice of words.

"Well, then," Scarlett said with a smile as Baxter had brought her back to her senses, an antidote to Hunter's spell. Thank goodness. She wasn't particularly fond of Baxter — certainly not as she was of Lavinia — but she hadn't spent much time with him save the odd dinner. He droned on and on about people and circumstances for which she had no care, nor did anyone else it seemed. She glanced over at Hunter, determining that Baxter was not in his own particular good graces. Although that could have been more to do with Baxter's timing than the man himself. "I suppose we best get on with it. Ah, Mrs. Shepherd!" she called, seeing the housekeeper pass by. Was that a grin the rotund woman was suppressing? Scarlett looked at her with some suspicion, but Mrs. Shepherd was the picture of innocence as she stopped and folded her hands together in front of her.

"Yes, my lady?"

"As Lord Keppel is joining us to light the Yule log, perhaps Lavinia would like to be present as well," she said, and Hunter's slight groan from beside her made her smile. "Would you mind informing her?"

The housekeeper's smile fell. Why, Scarlett had no idea.

"Actually, Mrs. Shepherd," she said, warming to the idea. "Why do we not have all the servants present?"

"What?" Baxter asked incredulously, waving around an unlit cheroot. "What do you mean to invite the *servants*? Oxford, tell your wife not to be ridiculous."

"Actually, Keppel, I think it is a fine idea," Hunter said with some relish, and when Scarlett looked over at him, he gave her a warm smile. He was simply getting a rise out of

Baxter, she knew, but she appreciated his support all the same.

Hunter picked up the Yule log from where he had discarded it before their sudden embrace, hefting it into his arms. It really was the perfect log, and Scarlett appreciated Hunter's patience with her. She followed him as he set it upon the embers burning low in the grate.

It was the perfect setting. The stone of the fireplace, likely picked from these very lands, bordered the grate itself. The mantel was now lined with greenery, and the room began to fill as curious maids and enthusiastic footmen entered it. The staff here wasn't particularly large, but when they were all in one room, they were quite the little community.

Hunter welcomed them all but then stood awkwardly beside her, finally leaning over and whispering in her ear, his breath tickling the skin underneath, moving little whips of hair against her neck. "Is there anything I ... do?" he asked her, and she tried not to giggle. The man truly knew nothing about Christmas.

"Just light it and wish everyone a happy Christmas!" she said, softly enough so as not to embarrass him in front of the staff. He nodded, took hold of a match, and struck it, the flame beginning to rise in front of him. Tiny flames had already begun to lick the edges of the bark from the embers in the grate, but Hunter lit the top of it all the same. The wet bark began to smoke, but the thick log was dry inside and soon enough began to merrily burn.

"Thank you all for being here to witness the first Yule Log in Wintervale's recent history," he said with a smile for his staff. "I know it has been some time since I have been in residence, but I believe I have left you in good hands with my wife." Scarlett's cheeks warmed as the staff nodded enthusiastically, and Hunter sent a smile of appreciation her way through a sideways glance. "I appreciate each and every one of you, and wish you all a happy Christmas."

A smattering of applause began amongst the servants, who shortly thereafter began to filter out of the room to see to their duties. Lavinia and Baxter remained, looking slightly bemused.

"Hunter Tannon celebrating Christmas," said Lavinia as she strode toward them. "I never thought I would see the day."

"It's just a log, Nia," he muttered in response, surprising Scarlett as his face became shuttered. "It doesn't much matter."

"I would beg to disagree," his sister argued. "You are quite an influence, Scarlett. I'm impressed."

Scarlett shrugged, not understanding why it was so significant. Neither of them seemed to want to discuss it, however, and before long, they were making their way to one of the drawing rooms. Scarlett was going to change for the evening, but Lavinia insisted they would be leaving shortly after dinner, so not to go to any trouble. Looking down at the deep blue of her outdoor walking garment, Scarlett began to disagree, but when she strode past the blue drawing room toward her chambers, she caught sight of Marion with Spicer. Hunter's valet had his head bent low next to hers. They were cleaning the room of the remaining greenery and ribbon from earlier in the day, but it seemed they were much more interested in one another than the task at hand. Scarlett grinned. While she wasn't sure what the future might hold for the two of them, Spicer seemed to be a sweet young man, and if this was what Marion wanted, then Scarlett hoped she found in him what she was looking for. If nothing else, it would make for a lovely Christmas.

As for her own romance this season.... She slowed her steps as she returned to the main drawing room, where Hunter and his family awaited her. She hadn't wanted this. She had expressly kept herself as far from Hunter as possible, turning him away at every turn. Yet, somehow he had managed to find his way through the thick shell she had built around herself, becoming far too intimate with not only her body but her thoughts.

While he would be returning to London soon, it wasn't the last she would see of him. This man would be with her, at one point or another, for the rest of their lives. She was longing to allow him into her heart, but she knew when he left it would only break it clean in two. *A few more days*, she thought with new resolve. *Just find your way through the next few days and all will be as it was.*

Only she knew that things would never be the same again.

HUNTER PACED in front of Scarlett's room. His sister and her husband had finally left, thank goodness. What they thought was a quick dinner had turned into an evening of reluctant entertainment. Damn Baxter Shaw. Hunter never enjoyed the man's company, but today had been something else entirely. Had he not entered the room when he did, Hunter could now be in bed with his wife, enjoying the consummation of his marriage that had been so long in coming.

Did he go to Scarlett now? His body screamed at him to knock down the door and take her, as her body responded to him with more willingness than any other woman he had ever been in company with.

But tonight, when he had said goodnight to her, looking deep into her eyes with a promise of more, her hazel eyes had been dark and shuttered.

"Goodnight, Hunter," she had said, turning from him at the divide between their rooms without any further invitation. Did he attempt to go to her, or would he only be rejected? He could only take so much of it from her. Perhaps he was pushing too hard, too fast. For he didn't simply want her to open to him physically, but he yearned for her to share more of herself with him.

He didn't have much time, however, until he would make his return to London. He wished he knew how he could convince her to come with him, to truly be his wife, but she seemed quite settled here. He would ask her in the morning. Everything would be well — tomorrow. It was Christmas, and, he had been told, Christmas was a day for miracles.

12

————

"Good morning, my lord," Spicer entered Hunter's rooms the next day humming that cheerful tune again.

"Good morning, Spicer," he replied groggily. Hunter had never woken easily, taking some time to ease out of slumber.

"Your coffee," Spicer said, bringing a tray around the bed, and Hunter took it gratefully.

"You're a saint, Spicer," he said, as he did every morning, though Spicer's laugh seemed slightly more jovial today than it did most days. "You're in good spirits this morning."

"Of course — it's Christmas, my lord! Happy Christmas!"

Hunter shrugged. It was Christmas, true, but it was simply another day, though one in which he went to church and had yet another dinner with his sister. And — oh yes — this year, it was the day in which he must convince his wife that she should be happy to be married to him.

Spicer continued to whistle as he went to the wardrobe and began to choose Hunter's clothing. Hunter looked over at him with narrowed eyes.

"Has anything ... occurred, Spicer?" He had given Scarlett a hard time about her preoccupation with the servants' affairs, but now here he was, questioning his valet like a young girl tittering about the latest love affair. What the hell was wrong with him? "Never mind," he said, waving a hand in the air. "Has any post been able to come through?"

"It's, ah, Christmas Day, my lord," Spicer said apologetically, and Hunter sighed. Right. He felt like a bit of a beast as he looked at his young, eager valet. The lad had tried to wet down his own unruly hair, but pieces of it were standing straight at attention. Hunter gulped down a couple of sips of coffee.

"It's the lady's maid, isn't it?"

"Pardon me, my lord?"

"Your good spirits — they would be due to my wife's maid?"

"Marion," Spicer said, a smile stretching his face and a faraway look coming to his eyes. Hunter let out a low chuckle.

"Women will do that to you," he said, hearing the ruefulness in his tone.

"Ah, how long do you suppose we will stay in the country?" Spicer asked, looking up at him hopefully as he laid out Hunter's breeches and waistcoat.

"Until the roads are clear enough," Hunter said, pushing back the bedcovers and walking to the window. He set his coffee down on the windowsill as he drew on a robe. "It didn't snow overnight," he observed, "So as long as a fair amount of traffic comes through, in a day or so we should be back in London."

"Parliament will not resume until March, my lord, is that correct?" Spicer asked, and Hunter simply narrowed his eyes at him in response.

"Pardon me, my lord," his valet said, brushing an invisible piece of lint off of Hunter's jacket. "I simply like to be prepared, that is all."

Hunter raised an eyebrow. "Very well," he said. "A couple of days it will be, however, for I have business to attend to, lords I must meet, and ..." he couldn't think of anything else. He had been so desperate to return to London, but really, many of his peers would remain in the country. He had to meet with Lord Falconer, true, but that could easily be arranged or rearranged. Why was he defending his decision to his valet, anyway? Because he was leaving his wife and he was suffering from guilt as a result.

It was her own fault. She was more than free to come with him. And with that thought on his mind, he dressed and went down for breakfast.

SCARLETT GREETED Hunter as he strode into the breakfast room. She was actually slightly surprised he hadn't come to her last night, though relieved he didn't, for she had no idea how she would have responded to him. Her body desperately called to him, but even thinking of it made her heart pound. For she was afraid. Afraid that if she truly gave herself to him, he wouldn't just break through her walls but would shatter them completely and she would be a ghost of her mother, spending the rest of her days trailing around Wintervale, waiting for her husband to come home and bestow upon her the slightest bit of attention.

She shook off the melancholy thoughts, determined to enjoy this one day, a day that her mother, despite her own hardships, had always been adamant Scarlett celebrate to its fullest.

"Happy Christmas," she said, and his eyebrows raised in surprise.

"Ah, yes," he responded. "Happy Christmas."

"What would you like to do this Christmas Day?"

"Do?" he asked, his eyebrows rising near to his hairline.

"Yes!" she said with a laugh. "I know the church service is later, but I thought perhaps we could go for a ride this morning, then maybe read for a while this afternoon. I know it's not much of a tradition, but it's what my mother and I always used to do."

"And your father?" Hunter asked. "Where was he within the merriment?"

Scarlett's grin faded. "He wasn't around," she said, not wanting to speak of it on this day that was to be of joy, and she idly fingered her locket. "Well," she said, placing her napkin on the table. "I'll be in the stables if you—"

"Won't you let me eat my bacon first?" The pleading look he constructed was so earnest that she had to laugh, and so she sat and kept him company while he ate. She had to admit that he was more than amiable when he didn't have anything distracting him. With correspondence undeliverable and his work suspended for a moment, she had his full attention, and it was lovely to be appreciated.

"There is one other thing," she said as he drank the last of his coffee. He looked at her with question. "You had mentioned that you may be interested in supporting some of my charitable work."

"Ah, yes!" he said, his eyes brightening, and she knew that while he maintained the same enthusiasm, he had completely forgotten. "Of course. What do you require?"

"I'd like my own account, completely for charity where I see fit," she began, listing one of her ideas. "There are villagers and tenants who sometimes need an extra hand. I know of Stone's concern regarding favoritism, but that is not the case, Hunter. They know when someone needs help and would, in fact, help one another if they could. The tenants will wish no ill will upon one another, I'm sure of it."

"Very well," he said, nodding, and then beckoned her to follow him into his study. She sat across from him on the other side of his large mahogany desk as he began to make a list on the tabletop in front of him. "Account," he said, taking the quill pen from his desk, dipping it in ink and beginning to scratch on the parchment. "Next!" he said, sitting up tall, his curls flopping over his forehead. Scarlett hid a laugh behind her hand at his animation.

She cleared her throat. "There is a charity in London, run by a friend of mine and her husband. It benefits women and children who have nowhere else to go. I'd like to direct funds to them as well."

"Very good," he said, writing it down with the particulars.

"And the hospital," she added eagerly. "They certainly need whatever can be given."

"I've heard many enjoy volunteering there as well," he said, and she looked at him suspiciously but said nothing. Was he trying to encourage her to come to London as a volunteer?

"Many do," she said cryptically, but after a pause, she added warmly, "Thank you, Hunter. This truly is a wonderful Christmas gift."

"A gift?" he looked up at her with confusion knotting his eyebrows together.

"Of course. And I have something for you in return."

"You needn't have done that."

"Oh, it's nothing much at all," she said, reaching into her pocket. "Here."

"You shouldn't have gotten anything for me."

"I wanted to," she said, her cheeks warming. Hopefully he didn't read anything into this or assume it was more than what she had meant. It was a Christmas gift, that was all. She had prepared gifts for the tenants and the staff — she figured she should have something for her husband.

"I, ah, I don't have anything for you," he said with a grimace. "I've never celebrated Christmas before, and so I didn't ... I just didn't know."

"It's fine," she assured him. "You've done enough."

He looked as though he was going to argue with her, but she pushed the small package toward him. He glanced at her with hesitation in his gaze, but at her encouraging nod, he began to pull apart the twine. The paper fell away to reveal a small box. Upon opening it, a gold pocket watch peered up at him.

He paused for a moment before gently picking it up, turning it over in his hands as he stared at it.

Scarlett shifted awkwardly in her chair. Why wasn't he saying anything?

"I'm not sure if you still want it, after what you said about never receiving one as a gift, nor choosing to carry one," she began, trying to explain herself. "But I noticed that at our wedding breakfast, you were worried about the time, and you didn't seem to have anything on you. I figured if you were a man of importance within the House of Lords, you should know what time it is so that you never miss anything. Although I suppose you have your servants to tell you, so maybe..."

"It's perfect."

His voice was so low she had to lean closer to hear him. "Truly?"

"Truly." His smile was hesitant, trembling, and yet warm.

He seemed disarmed, and the slight blush that covered his face made him look nearly boyish, years younger than he was.

"I don't know why I never carried one," he mused, his eyes faraway now, looking over her shoulder at nothing and yet everything at the same time. "It was stubbornness, I suppose. I always thought a pocket watch was typically something you do receive as a gift, or as an heirloom passed down from one generation to the next. After asking for one and never receiving it, my father never deigning to give me such a thing, not when he could keep it for himself, and my mother not even thinking of us when it came to such things, well, I never did bring myself to buy one for myself. Silly, really...."

His voice trailed off, as he was clearly lost in his thoughts, speaking to himself as much as he was to her.

"Anyway," he said with more emphasis, coming back to himself and their conversation. "Thank you, Scarlett, truly. Ah, the time is even accurate!"

"I wound it for you," she said, averting her gaze from his when it became too pointed, too intense. She cleared her throat. "Well, if you are nearly finished, let's go out of doors now, shall we? The sun is shining merrily and while it will be cold, we can then have chocolate prepared for us when we return. Very well?"

"Very well," he said, and Scarlett couldn't quite read his expression as he sat back and looked at her. Finally, he simply cleared his throat. "Fancy a race?"

He had hardly finished his sentence when she was up, out of her chair, and already flying toward the stables. He chuckled and started after her.

13

———

Hunter dressed with immaculate care that night. Why, he wasn't sure. Scarlett was already his wife — he shouldn't need to go to great pains to impress her.

And yet, he longed for nothing more than for her to look at him with the same enthusiasm she did everyone else who came into her life — and that damn Yule log.

"You look very dapper, my lord," said Spicer as he finished smoothing the final crease in Hunter's cravat.

Hunter grinned at his valet. "Thank you, Spicer," he said. "I have you to thank, of course."

"I must say, that is a tremendous pocket watch."

"It is, isn't it?"

Hunter lifted the gold plated watch in his hand, turning it round and round. He noticed something then on the back of it, an inscription he hadn't seen previously. He moved over to the sconce, holding the watch up to the candlelight.

December 25, 1813.

Today's date. She had planned this long before she even knew he would be home, before she even knew his story of wishing for one. Guilt tugged at his heart then, for if the snow hadn't fallen as it did, he would be back in London, leaving her here alone on Christmas Day. Would she have given him the watch? Or sold it elsewhere? He could hardly ask her without breaking the little trust they were beginning to build. As it was, she had given it to him only to aid in his work in London, not to arrive home in time for dinner — for she apparently had no plans on being in his townhouse awaiting him.

He placed the watch back in his pocket, his heart warming at the first true gift he had ever received. He supposed Lavinia would have given him something in the past, had she herself been used to the custom of giving and receiving. But alas, that notion had never been a part of their cold childhood.

"You'll be heading to church then?" Spicer asked, and at Hunter's nod, he found his cloak and gloves and laid them on the bed.

"It's become mighty cold, my lord," he said, "but I believe the path is clear enough to the village for the horses and sleigh. Just have to hope it doesn't snow much between now and then."

"We shall have to hope, Spicer," he replied and went out to find his wife.

Perhaps she was the one requiring a pocket watch, he thought minutes later as he waited for her in Stone Hall. If she took any longer, they would be late for the church service. He was about to find Mrs. Shepherd to ask her to collect his wife when he heard footsteps on the stairs above him. He looked up, at first noticing the step he heard was from her hard black boot, for it would be foolish to go out of doors in the little kid slippers she loved.

But his gaze quickly traveled upward, and his heart

seemed to stop as he took her in from her toes to the top of her head.

She was extraordinary. Breathtaking. He had known it before, of course, but there was something about her at this moment that he couldn't put a finger on.

Her green dress was wide around her shoulders, the gold embroidered edges bordering her delicate collarbones, joining together at the bodice in the middle, a gold tucker covering most of her breasts, the tops of the tiny mounds showing just enough to tempt him as his eyes rested upon her. A gold braid emphasized her narrow waist, from where the green of her skirts billowed out to wave around her ankles, a gold petticoat peeking out from underneath.

As beautiful as her dress was, it was her face that held him. Her chestnut hair with its highlights of cinnamon was piled high on her head, with pieces falling softly around her face, drawing his attention to her sculpted cheekbones and the hazel eyes that held his. She bit her full bottom lip, the rosy red of it beckoning him to run up the stairs as fast as he was able and take them under his. He held himself back, however, as he felt the presence of servants gathering behind him.

"Beautiful," he heard Spicer breathe, and if Hunter were able to tear his eyes away from his wife, he would have glared at him with all of the jealousy and possessiveness of a man in love.

For he was. He loved her. Despite the wall of ice she had built around herself, he had come to know this woman over the past couple of days — which was foolish in itself, to fall in love with someone after a two-day acquaintance. And yet, he had. Any frostiness remaining around her was simply there to protect herself. Warmth was what truly emanated from her, was part of her very soul. The few times she had bestowed upon him a glimpse into the woman underneath, she stirred something within him that he had never known was there.

She finally resumed her slow march down the stairs toward him, her eyes never leaving his until she was a step above him.

"You look beautiful," he finally breathed, and she simply smiled up at him.

"Hunter green." He heard the whisper behind him, and he turned his head to see Scarlett's lady's maid had joined them in the entryway. Did she just wink at him? No, he shook his head. Surely, she wouldn't. But he certainly didn't miss the impish smile on her face as she took the hand of his valet and led him out of the room.

"You look beautiful this evening, my lady," Mrs. Shepherd finally said, breaking the silence, and his butler nodded as well, holding out his arm, upon which their cloaks were draped.

"You best be going or you'll miss the service," he said. "We will be along shortly behind you. Your sister awaits in the sleigh in the drive. I know she has invited you for dinner, but if you choose to return home — because of the weather of course — Cook has promised to have a fine Christmas meal prepared."

"We will be home," Hunter said, his voice thick.

"Very good, my lord!" His butler and housekeeper looked thrilled, though why they cared, he wasn't sure.

"What?" Scarlett asked, surprise registering on her face.

"I said we will be home after mass," he repeated as he steered her out the door. No more games, no more visitors, no more intrusions.

Tonight, his wife would become his.

Scarlett kept stealing glances at her husband throughout the church service. She had been to the village church every Sunday morning without fail since she took up residence at Wintervale, but tonight, the church had been transformed. The copper brick walls had turned a dusky amber with the glow of the candlelight from the sconces that lined the building. The choir's tones were hushed and melodic, celebrating the joy of the baby born so many years ago, the air filled with the smell of straw upon which a porcelain collection of shepherds, wise men, livestock, and Mary and Joseph themselves gathered around the baby Jesus.

But for Scarlett, it was more than the warm, cheerful atmosphere that surrounded her. It was the man beside her. Something had changed within Hunter, though she wasn't sure what it was or what had caused it. His usual nonchalant air was gone, replaced by a man with determination written all over his face. His jaw was tight, his cheekbones pronounced, his eyebrows drawn together.

One thing *was* certain — she had never seen a more handsome man in her entire life. He may not have celebrated many Christmases before, but he certainly knew how to dress for one.

When she had walked down the stairs of Stone Hall toward him, his blue-green eyes had turned from their usual warmth to a shade darker somehow as they focused so intensely upon her. If only she knew what he was thinking. She wanted to ask, but for once in her life, she was too nervous. For his answer could change everything between them, and she wasn't altogether sure she wanted that.

In fact, she thought as the congregation rose for the mass to begin, she had no idea what she wanted any longer.

A multitude of emotions curdled in her stomach, as she both longed for her husband as well as feared what could happen if he were to leave her. *When* he would leave her, that was, for he was surely returning to London in due time.

She looked down at her lap, seeing his broad, strong hand just inches from hers. If theirs was a different relationship, she would only have to lift her hand and bring it down upon his for his warm touch to suffuse her. But she couldn't — not now, despite how much she yearned to be closer to him. As it was, they were pressed close together in the tight pew due to the filled church, and every time he moved, she had to shut her eyes for a moment as his hard body against hers sent all kinds of shivers through her.

She swallowed hard, looking at him out of the corner of her eye, and used all of her power to focus on the service and not on her husband.

SCARLETT COULDN'T REMEMBER mass ever being quite so long. The moment the last hymn concluded, Hunter jumped up, took her hand, and began leading her to the door as fast as he was able to reasonably move.

"Hunter—" she began, catching sight of Lavinia waving at them from across the church. Wintervale was between Lavinia's home and the village, so she and Baxter had insisted on collecting them.

Hunter turned and waved to his sister before pointing to the door. Lavinia, wanting to visit, pouted but Hunter shook his head, and Scarlett was amused by the unspoken argument between brother and sister.

Finally, Lavinia threw up her hands, took her husband by the arm, and led him to the door while Hunter had already pulled Scarlett through and was donning his fur hat.

"Hunter!" she admonished him once she finally caught up with the two of them, pushing up her glasses as they had apparently fallen down her nose in her haste to follow after them. "What is the rush? I was simply speaking with—"

"We have to get home."

"Whatever for?"

They stepped out into the cold night air, which was now filled with swirling snowflakes.

"For we must return before the snow leaves us stranded here in the village. Do you not see how thick and fast it is coming down?"

Scarlett turned around in a circle, ascertaining that Hunter was, indeed, correct. Snow was beginning to collect upon the thatched roofs surrounding them, icicles hanging from their eaves. She couldn't help herself. She threw her arms out, let her head hang back, and opened her mouth to collect snowflakes as they descended toward her.

"Scarlett! What in heaven's name are you doing?" asked Lavinia, although Scarlett could hear the laughter in her voice.

"Collecting snowflakes!" she exclaimed, raising her head to look at her sister-in-law. "Did you never do such a thing?"

"No!" Lavinia said somewhat incredulously. "Our parents would have seen it as quite ... improper."

"Well, I suppose it is," said Scarlett with a shrug. "Though Hunter is right. We best be going."

"Did I hear you correctly?" he asked with a teasing look of astonishment. "I believe you just said I'm right."

"Well," she admitted, "for once you are."

He held a hand out to help her into the waiting sleigh, and despite the layers of gloves between them and the frigid night air, a jolt of heat coursed through her from where they touched right to her very center. *Get a hold of yourself Scarlett*, she thought as she sat next to him underneath the blanket keeping out the cold.

"So..." Lavinia began speaking before she was even fully inside, ignoring her husband who had already rummaged in his pocket to pull out a flask before the sleigh even began to move. "You will come for dinner tonight, will you not?"

"No," Hunter said curtly before turning his gaze toward the passing landscape. Lavinia's smile fell, and Scarlett leaned forward.

"We would love to Lavinia, truly we would," she said with much more tact. "However, we are concerned about the weather, and we wouldn't like to impose upon you overnight."

"Of course you may!" she exclaimed, but Hunter was already shaking his head.

"I'd like to spend Christmas alone with my wife," he said pointedly, shocking them all into silence with the exception of Baxter, who choked on his drink.

"Very well, then," said Lavinia, her eyebrows raised but a smug smile crossing her face. "We will leave you alone. But do come tomorrow instead?"

Scarlett simply nodded, and when the sleigh slid into Wintervale, Lavinia leaned back into the cushion behind her. "Have a lovely evening."

14

———

They had just entered the foyer, the heavy wooden door swinging shut behind them, when Hunter decided he had had enough of this bloody awkwardness between them. He was about to take Scarlett upstairs right then and there, but he stopped suddenly when he caught sight of her face, as it was full of wonder, fixed on the room in front of her.

"What in the..." her voice trailed off and he followed her gaze, beginning to stride forward with an arm at her back as she walked next to him wordlessly.

For strewn across the oak hardwood floors were evergreen needles and white and red petals — from what type of flower, he had no idea, although he was sure they were from his conservatory — lining the path before them through the oak-paneled hall, leading into the dining room. Spicer and Marion suddenly appeared, holding out their arms to divest them of their cloaks.

"Spicer," Hunter ground out, "what is the meaning of this?"

"Just a bit of Christmas cheer, my lord," he said quietly.

Hunter noticed Scarlett send a look of incredulity toward her maid, but Marion simply winked. Dazed, the two of them continued on into the dining room, finding Mrs. Shepherd and Abbot awaiting them, large smiles on their faces. Had his staff gone mad?

"Good evening, my lord, my lady," Mrs. Shepherd greeted them. "Mass was lovely, wasn't it? We will leave you now. We simply wanted to ensure all was well. We hope you have a lovely dinner."

Hunter looked over to Scarlett, seeing that she shared his surprise and suspicion.

"Abbot," he said before his butler could clear the doorway. "Do you care to share what is occurring here?"

"It is Christmas, my lord," his butler said with a small smile. "And it's about time you celebrated it properly."

And they were gone with a click of the door handle, leaving Scarlett and Hunter alone in the dining room. Except it no longer looked like the dining room that he knew. A rich crimson tablecloth covered only one end of the long dining table, with a straight-backed chair placed at the head of it, another just beside, their curved legs seeming to reach toward one another as they framed the corner of the table.

The table settings were intimately close, the only light besides the fire was a few lit candles, while the heavily gilt Chippendale chandelier hanging over the table in bold outlines and delicate detail remained dark. While the room was dim, it was also somehow warm and inviting. Hunter turned to Scarlett, holding out his elbow. "It seems, Scarlett, our servants had plans of their own for us tonight."

Her lips twitched at his suggestion, but she nodded, and if he didn't know better, he could have sworn that a blush rose in her cheeks. He held his arm out, and she slipped her hand into the crook of his elbow, her long, slender fingers gripping his upper arm.

Hunter looked down at the top of her head, but all he could see were her curled tresses as she kept her face turned away from him, facing out toward the feast that awaited. The only noise was the sound of their booted feet on the oak floor as they walked toward the table. Through the window, stars twinkled in the dark sky overhead, creating a shimmering backdrop on this Christmas night.

Hunter pulled out Scarlett's seat, purposely brushing his fingertips along the satiny skin of the back of her neck as he pushed her chair in slightly behind her, and he could feel her shiver underneath his touch, though she said nothing.

When he took his seat, he brought his chair in even closer to her so that their knees rested against each other, his foot sitting between hers. She chewed her lip, her eyes flitting from one side to the other, and he could sense her trying to decide what to do next. She had an unconscious tendency to worry strands of hair round and round her fingers, despite what it did to the state of whichever hairstyle he was sure her maid had painstakingly concocted. Now, she pulled on the strands that were falling low, nearly to her breasts, the tops of which were peeking out of her bodice, beckoning to him. Clearly, she had no idea what she was doing to him.

Finally her spicy eyes became hooded, and it seemed that her body won the internal war being waged within her as she leaned on her elbows closer toward him.

"So ... Hunter," she said slowly, raising her eyes to meet his. "What do you think of Christmas so far?"

"I think," he said, reaching out to pick up the wine which had been waiting in front of him, and satisfaction coursed through him when he saw her swallow as she watched his fingers rub the edge of the glass. "It has been altogether surprising," he said.

"You seem ... different tonight," she said somewhat nervously.

He sat back in his chair, contemplating her. Her chestnut hair was still in its elaborate style, though more strands had fallen down over her shoulders and chest. As she ran her fingers through a strand, he wanted nothing more than to replace her hand with his own — but he stopped himself as he didn't want to scare her.

Over the last couple of days, he had learned that his wife was one who didn't hesitate to take a risk, to put herself ahead of any fears or concerns she might have. He didn't expect her to back down from him, but he also wasn't sure what type of reaction to expect from her. Would she accept him and all he offered her, or would her guard come up and would she push him away once more?

"I suppose you could say that the Christmas spirit has come over me."

"Oh?" she said, raising an eyebrow. "And what is it that has so enthralled you?"

"Well," he drawled. "I believe it began with the ride through the snow, followed by the snowball fight in the woods. Then it continued with our sleigh ride, your idea to present the tenants with gifts. And finally, the decorations, the Yule log, the church service, and, of course, the mistletoe."

"The mistletoe?"

"Yes," he said, winking at her, "the mistletoe."

He had rendered her speechless, for she sat there staring at him with her mouth open. The truth was, it wasn't the snow, nor the gifts, nor the decoration, nor even the bloody mistletoe that had warmed him to Christmas. It was her.

She filled the house and his life with laughter and joy, and he didn't want to let her go. If only he could have her bestow some of that same spirit upon himself — even a little — his life would never be the same. But first, he had to convince her to trust him, to even learn to like him enough that perhaps they could find a way forward as true husband and wife.

And if Christmas made her happy, then so be it.

In the moment of silence, he began to hear the stirrings of a song.

"Do you hear..."

"Music," she finished, and they both turned and looked out the door in an effort to determine where it was coming from.

"Stone Hall," he finally said.

"Pardon me?"

"It's coming from Stone Hall. We may not be directly connected to the door, but we share a wall, and it holds the best pianoforte in the house," he said, his smile beginning to grow. Who was playing the instrument, he had no idea, although he guessed it was likely Marion, as he doubted whether many of the maids would possess the skill to play it. "Our staff has certainly set the scene."

"Yes," Scarlett agreed as a footman hurried over to fill her empty wine glass. "They certainly have."

There was a moment of silence as the first course of soup was placed in front of them. Scarlett began to stir it, metal tings ringing out from her spoon on the bowl until she finally brought the soup to her mouth.

"Why did you come back?" she asked suddenly, her words coming out in a rush, and the look that rose to meet his was hesitant, vulnerable, as though asking had cost her much of her pride.

"Well," he said slowly, wanting to tell her the truth of it while at the same time needing her to understand how important it was that she was here with him, that she remained with him.

"I received the notice from Stone regarding the funds," he said, clearing his throat. "So I thought it best to come see to matter myself. And I'm glad I did," he mused. "The man will be gone after Christmastide, that I can promise you. I apologize for not believing you sooner."

"Was that the only reason you came?"

She looked so hopeful, so expectant, but Hunter didn't want to lie to her. And yet ... as he stared at his wife, he realized there was more to his desire for honesty. He longed to know her, to see if there was a chance for the two of them. Initially he had set out to woo her because socially, he needed a wife, and an heir would be required at some point — it made sense of a man in his position. But now that he had come to know her better, he yearned for her, not because she was his wife and a woman he would be bonded together with for life, but because she was intriguing. She was kind. She was generous. And she was sexy as hell.

Did she know that when she leaned in as she was now, she was giving him a full view of her breasts? Probably not, and he wasn't going to say anything.

"No, that was not the only reason," he said gruffly. "While his summons is what provided me with the impetuous to return, there was more to it. I was hoping to convince you to be my wife in more than name, to return to London with me."

He could read her through her eyes, the way they darkened when she was angry, or when the gold in them sparked when she was pleased, as she had been when he began his sentence, though she looked down at her soup now, shutting them off from him completely at his words regarding his return.

"I am not returning to London."

"Let's not speak of it now," he said, not wanting to argue. He reached across the table and covered one of her hands with his. "At the moment, we're here together. It's Christmas. And we have much to celebrate."

"Oh?"

"Indeed," he said, his lips widening in a suggestive smile. The footmen came and went, removing the soup course and replacing it with goose. Hunter found the knife and began to slice it, plucking a piece from the serving tray and placing it on Scarlett's plate.

"I believe we have made progress," he continued. "You no longer run from the room when I enter. You actually respond to me when I speak to you. And, Scarlett, I think you may actually be feeling something for me."

She started at that, nearly jumping out of her chair.

"Why would you think that?" she asked, her voice just over a whisper.

"You haven't turned me away. You haven't run."

"I want to."

"Why?"

"Because..." Her voice broke slightly.

The goose forgotten between them, Hunter surreptitiously waved away the footmen, who nodded and slipped out the door into Oak Hall. Hunter picked up Scarlett's hand, which was still underneath his, clasping it, palm to palm, wrapping his fingers around it in silent encouragement for her to share more with him.

"Because I decided that even you, Hunter Tannon, deserve a Christmas gift." She grinned, and confusion spread through Hunter at her obvious coverage of what she had been about to say. She continued to deliberately avoid him, to push him away — but why? Though he supposed he should take the teasing, jesting wife over the sullen and cold one she had been before.

"I'm a lucky man, then," he said, squeezing her fingers, "for I have received not only my gift of a pocket watch, but my wife as well."

Her eyes flashed at him as she seemed to understand what he was saying and a slight smile crossed her face.

He had come to realize that smile was part of her defense, and he wasn't surprised when she leaned back from him, pulling her hand away. Her emotions were guarded once more, but he had made inroads into her thoughts, had begun to develop a connection that — he hoped — would only strengthen over time.

"Do you fancy some dessert?" she asked.

Did he ever.

15

_____

Because I don't want to fall in love with you and spend the rest of my life like my mother.

The truth had been on the tip of her tongue. Just as the words had been about to cross her lips, however, she caught herself, coming to the sudden realization of just how close she had allowed herself to grow to him. She was moments away from allowing him to see into her most innermost thoughts, which would have been the most foolhardy decision she could have made. But it seemed that the more she tried to push him away, the more she enjoyed his company, looked forward to the next time that they would see one another.

What was she doing, flirting with him, spending all of these precious moments alone together? Christmas was magical, but behind every magic trick was a practical explanation. In this case, it was simply the fact that the two of them were ensconced alone in this estate, with a staff apparently intent on them finding their way together.

"I suppose dessert can be arranged," he said, calling out

the door for a footman, who entered moments later with a tray of gingerbread, fruit cake, and bowls of plum pudding.

"My goodness," said Scarlett, her eyes widening. "If we eat all of this, we shall not be able to walk out of the room on our own two feet. I believe my stays may spring open."

"I can help you untie them if you'd like."

Scarlett whipped her gaze from the dessert to Hunter's face and found he was laughing at her, the corners of his eyes crinkling as a wide smile stretched across his face.

"You're a brute," she whispered sardonically.

He shrugged, winking at her. "I jest."

"I know."

"Here," he said, breaking their joined gaze, reaching down to scoop up a spoonful of pudding. He held it up toward her.

"While I have never had a Christmas feast as it were, every Christmas since I was a boy, Cook would ensure this was our dessert on Christmas Day. It's unlike anything you have ever tasted before, I promise."

"I'm not sure..." she said, as she had been eyeing the gingerbread.

"You must try the pudding," he insisted, and he looked so eager she finally gave in.

"Fine," she said with a sigh, reaching out to take the spoon from him.

"Ah, ah, no, allow me," he said, bringing the spoon to her lips. She opened wide for him, and his eyes sparked with undisguised desire. She hadn't time to digest the thought, however, as the pudding touched her tongue.

"Oh!" she said, bringing her napkin to her lips. "That is ... that is..."

"Vile?" he finished, his words dissolving into a chuckle.

"Yes, Cook has always had trouble with that particular recipe."

"Oh, you ... you..." She swatted his arm, and he laughed even harder.

"Have you run out of names for me? Ah, the look on your face right now," he said, mirth overcoming him.

She shook her head, narrowing her eyes at him. "That was rather unkind."

"It was worth it."

"Time for your own bite."

"Good Lord, no."

"Tell you what," she said with a grin. "I challenge you to a game of billiards. Whoever loses must eat the rest of the pudding."

He cocked his head to the side, and Scarlett was sure he was currently underestimating her.

"Very well," he said with a nod. "This should be fun."

Oh, she didn't doubt that. Her husband was in for a surprise.

He pushed his chair back from the table, before helping her from her own seat and taking the tray with him as he led her into the adjoining billiards room. A small yet cheery fire was the only light in the well-proportioned room, though the footman hurried in behind them to stoke the fire and light a few of the sconces that lined the wall. The flames flickered across the beautiful Gobelins tapestries that lined the room, their bright colors transporting the two of them to another world, a world beyond these walls or this country. Scarlett loved this room and had spent more time in here over the past few months than she would care to admit to Hunter, for then he would be aware that he might not so easily best her in a game of billiards.

Hunter placed the tray on a side table, from which he

filled a glass with amber liquid, holding it out to her first. She walked over to him, her swishing skirts the only sound in the room besides the crackle of the fire.

She took a hearty sip from the glass and passed it back, before removing two cue sticks from the wall. She gave one to Hunter, who set down the drink and arranged the balls in their correct place in the middle of the red velvet tabletop.

"Ladies first," he said, and she made a play of nearly missing the white cue ball.

"Oh, dear," she said distressingly, "It seems I am out of practice."

"Not to worry," he said reassuringly as he came around the table. "You'll pick up on it, I'm sure."

He easily sank five of his balls before finally missing one. Scarlett picked up her cue stick once more.

"Here," he said, looking at her with an easy grin, one she knew was sympathetic to her apparent plight. "Allow me."

He came around behind her, his arms encircling her as his warm hands covered hers. She had removed her gloves when they came into the house, for which she was glad as she enjoyed the feeling of his big warm hands on hers.

"Back and forth," Hunter said softly in her ear as he moved the cue with her. She shivered as his breath brushed across her neck, his body moving with hers, and heat suffused her, which had nothing to do with the temperature of the room.

"That's it," he said, allowing her to take over. "You've got this."

She nodded jerkily and he released her, leaving her slightly bereft as he walked away from her to round the table. He leaned over the side, his arms crossed as he concentrated on her.

She skirted around the table so he wasn't in her line of

sight, distracting her from her task at hand. She leaned over the red velvet, eyed the cue ball, and then connected with it square in the center, sending it toward its target and knocking the ball into its hole.

Hunter clapped his hands. "Well done!" he said, and Scarlett kept the chuckle from escaping her lips, not wanting to disappoint him, so proud he seemed by the effect of his instructions.

She smiled abstractly, wandering slowly over to his side of the table. She bent over it, feeling contact behind her as she did. He moved away, albeit rather slowly, one hand on the top of her back as he took a step from her.

She connected with the next ball, sinking it once more. Hunter blinked at her before narrowing his eyes. She simply smiled sweetly again, before knocking in the rest of her balls in quick succession.

"What in the..."

"I win," she said matter-of-factly as she replaced her cue stick. "I hope you are hungry for Cook's pudding."

"You tricked me!" he exclaimed, astonishment now covering his face.

"I did nothing of the sort," she said, shrugging a shoulder. "I never claimed any skill or lack thereof. You assumed what you wanted to."

"Good grief," he said, grimacing as he walked over to the sideboard. He took a big spoonful of the pudding, closing his eyes before sticking it into his mouth. He washed it down with a swig of brandy.

"Here," said Scarlett, laughing at him, "Allow me." She scooped up another hearty morsel, stood on her tiptoes, and set the spoon in his mouth. She had to give him credit, for he was taking this quite well. After his third bite, however, she took pity on him.

"Close your eyes," she commanded, and he obeyed. This time she picked up a piece of gingerbread, and when he opened his mouth obligingly, she slipped in a leg from the cookie creature.

"Mmm," he murmured, opening his eyes and looking down at her. "What did I do to deserve that?"

"I figured you needed something sweet," she said, and when she caught his gaze, her mirth faded, to be replaced by a flood of awareness.

"One more?" he asked, cocking an eyebrow.

"Very well," she said, lifting the other leg of the gingerbread to his lips. He opened to her, but when she placed it in his mouth, his lips came around not only the cookie but her fingers as well. His tongue licked her index finger, and she gasped as a wave of heat shot from her hand to her very center. She had never felt anything like it, and God help her, she wanted to feel it again. He took her left hand in his, his fingers twining around hers.

Straightening, his hands came to her hips, and Scarlett, spellbound, went along with the current that pulled her into him, and when her body made contact with his, he lifted her up, placing her bottom on the velvet top. Her legs widened, and he stepped in between them, allowing her to feel him up against her. And oh, it felt good. He leaned in, his hand coming to the back of her head, his lips meeting hers in a dance she eagerly welcomed.

Their kiss had been brewing since the moment she walked down the stairs earlier this evening, and Scarlett was now both satisfied and desperate for more in equal parts. She drank in his taste, of brandy and gingerbread, as one hand came to the left side of his whiskered jaw, the other twining into the curls of his hair. They were as silky and as luscious as she had imagined, and she was grateful he didn't cut it in the latest fashion.

Don't do this, Scarlett. Don't give away your body and with it, your heart.

The thought flew into her mind, but as Hunter's lips slanted over hers again and again, his tongue tangling with hers, the words were pushed aside just as quickly, to be replaced by a need unlike anything she had ever felt before. He broke away, only to desperately whisper, "I think, my wife, it is time for bed."

Hunter picked her up as though she weighed nothing, one arm coming beneath her knees, the other around her back. He angled her through the door of the billiards room, skirting around the small statues and delicate furniture of Stone Hall, before striding up the stairs, while his ancestors watched on. Scarlett looked around at their portraits, wondering if that was approval in their eyes. She shook her head to relieve herself of her fanciful notions, tightening her arms around Hunter's neck. She had never seen a man so determined. When they came upon a startled housemaid in the upstairs corridor, Hunter ignored her gasp as he continued on his way. He turned the corner, finally coming to his own bedroom. He pushed the door open with his boot, and Scarlett's face flushed when she saw Spicer was inside, laying out his master's bedclothes.

"Out," was all Hunter said, and Scarlett attempted a smile of apology, though one didn't seem to be needed. Despite his attempts at smothering it, Spicer wore a grin at the sight of Scarlett in his lord's arms. He hurriedly scurried out of the room, likely to tell the rest of the staff, Scarlett thought, but at this point, she didn't care any longer.

Hunter tossed her on the bed, the cover a deep navy to match the curtains, which had been pulled over the windows, but for one through which Scarlett could see the very top of a snow-covered pine. The air between them now was so tense that when a log cracked in the fireplace, Scarlett nearly jumped off the bed. She was always one up for adventure, but this was something else entirely.

For whether she was sending her horse into a gallop across a grassy field, or plunging into one of London's most undesirable neighborhoods to give out baskets to mothers in need, *she* was in control. And tonight, she had completely given up every vestige of it to Hunter. Her husband.

As she looked on, he shed his jacket before unpinning his cravat, sending it flying through the air with a tug. Next, he removed his waistcoat, then moved his fingers to the top buttons of his shirt. Scarlett could watch no longer, however, as the power of her instincts overcame all else. She shifted to her knees, bringing herself to the edge of the bed and drawing Hunter toward her. As he stood looking down at her, she began to undo the buttons herself, clumsily at first until she began to understand the way of it.

She could feel the intensity of Hunter's stare as he watched her, and by the time she unfastened his final button, his patience apparently evaporated. He ripped the shirt over his head, before coming down upon her like a ferocious animal attacking its prey.

His lips descended on hers, hungrily tasting, demanding, telling her that he needed something more — as did she in equal measure.

"You," he said between kisses, "are wearing entirely too much clothing."

Not breaking their contact, he undid the buttons of the back of her gown much more deftly than she had his, before pushing down the green folds of the dress until her bosom was exposed. While he seemed insistent on undressing her, he was momentarily distracted by her breasts, and he showed her just how much he enjoyed them as he brought his mouth to one, circling the bud of her nipple with his tongue.

"Oh!" she cried out, having been previously unaware of the wondrous sensations his actions could provoke. He paused momentarily to divest her of the rest of her gown, flinging aside the gold and green creation.

"That," he said, "Is the loveliest packaging I have ever unwrapped."

Her chemise seemed to entirely disappear without her even noticing, and it seemed his hands were everywhere at once — from her breasts, down her ribcage, back up to her neck, in her hair, before grasping her hips. She arched toward him, needing something more to quench this fire that was burning within her. The rough fabric of his breeches scratched against her legs, and she began clawing at his fall to try to be rid of the material. His fingers brushed against hers as he took over, quickly shedding his breeches and stockings until they joined the growing pieces of clothing strewn about the room.

Any thoughts remaining fled when one of his magical hands came to her center, beginning to work all kinds of wonders. Something was growing, building inside of her, but she didn't want it like this. She yearned to know him, to be one with him.

"Hunter," she groaned. "I need you to ... to..." She knew what it was, but she wasn't entirely sure how to put it into words. Fortunately, he seemed to understand, for his fingers left her, to be replaced by something much harder stroking against her entrance.

"Scarlett," he groaned as he began to slide inside of her. "Scarlett, I love you."

16

Scarlett froze.

She could blame much of her momentary stillness for the pain. While it certainly didn't hurt nearly as much as others had told her, all the same it was a shock that she needed a moment to become accustomed to.

But more than that, it was Hunter's words of love. Did he mean it? Did he love her? Or was it simply words spoken in the throes of passion? Did she believe it? For if she did ... well, then she might have to admit the full extent of her own feelings, and she wasn't sure she was quite ready to do so, if she ever would be. For that was crossing a line she had told herself she was never going to cross. Did he expect her to say something in return? Her thoughts fled, however, when he began to move.

He was gentle at first, a slow in and out, but soon his pace picked up in a rhythm as old as time itself, and she allowed the ecstasy to overcome her. He reached down between them, finding the most sensitive spot of her body, playing with her until all of the sensations she had felt before he had cut into her consciousness with his words of love came roaring back. Her hands dug into the strong muscles of his buttocks as she ground herself against him, until finally the fire exploded within her, sparks shooting out through every part of her. She cried out on a half-sob, half-shout as Hunter quickened his pace before finally stilling, seeming to shake as he found his own release.

They stayed joined together for a moment more as they each recovered their breath, though Scarlett wasn't sure that her heart would ever return to its regular pace.

Eventually, he rolled off of her, coming to his back, arms spread wide on the bed. One reached out to her, curling around her shoulders as he brought her close to him, wedging her into his side. She rested her head on his chest, a hand coming up to feel the springy curls dusting over him.

She closed her eyes and swallowed, not wanting to admit her thoughts out loud, hardly able to even think them herself. She was falling in love with her husband.

HUNTER WOKE to sunshine streaming across his face, entering the room from the slight crack in the curtains. What time was it? He was typically awake and in his office reviewing the day's correspondence and background documents he needed knowledge of long before the sun arose in the winter months. He was, however, considerably tired this morning. And all because — because of her.

He looked down beside him. Scarlett's long, slightly wavy hair was strewn out over the pillow behind her head like a halo around the face of an angel. The sun danced across the scattering of freckles that covered her nose. Her mouth was open just slightly in sleep, enough that he could see the crooked bottom teeth through her plump lips. She was perfect.

Hunter reached out, running a finger along the soft, porcelain skin of her collarbone, across the locket she still wore, over her shoulder and down her arm, until he came to her hands, and he intertwined her fingers with his. She grunted a little in sleep, and he chuckled, smiling as she instinctively drew closer to him, throwing an arm across his torso.

This is what he had longed for since he had married the woman over three months ago. Despite the cold front she had initially presented to him, she was as warm as anyone he had ever met. She had held him at arm's length for so long, and he did understand her reasoning — she was wary at first, as was he. He had feared her rejection. When she refused to accept him, he had left as quickly as he could, unwilling to suffer the same denial of love he had his entire childhood. He should have given it more time, been more patient with her. For she had proven to be someone entirely different than who she had initially presented to him.

He thought back to the previous night. She had opened herself up to him, in more ways than just by giving him her body. And he had — had he told her he *loved* her? He thought perhaps he had, though a slight niggling of worry crept into his heart as he certainly didn't recall her saying anything back. *That* he would remember. Perhaps she had simply been too overcome to respond. That must be it. She would tell him how she felt in due time, he was sure of it.

Not wanting to wake her, Hunter eventually extricated his hand, finding his robe and pulling it on before leaving the room, shutting the door softly behind him. He made his way down the steps and was startled when a figure surprised him in the hall.

"Ah, Miss..."

"Parker, my lord."

"Miss Parker," he said, addressing Scarlett's maid. "Your lady is still sleeping but at some point she will require a change of clothes."

"Very good, my lord," she said, and just when she began down the corridor, the maid's sitting room door opened, and out stepped his valet.

"My lord!" Spicer said, running a hand through his hair. "I, ah, that is, I—"

"Good morning, Spicer," Hunter said, happy his valet had found love just as he had himself. He continued down the hall, whistling a tune. It would be a fine day today. A very fine day indeed.

HUNTER DIDN'T KNOW how long he sequestered himself away in his office, pausing only long enough to change quickly, finding Scarlett gone from his bed. The post had finally come through. The snow had paused, momentarily at least, though the freezing temperatures remained. Soon enough it would be time to return to London, and for the first time the thought was accompanied by a sense of melancholy rather than excitement or even impatience. His time here with Scarlett had been a pause in his regular life, and Hunter wasn't sure he wanted to go back.

But he had no choice. For there was much to be done, from discussion of the war with Boney to the changes he wanted to take action on, which he couldn't do if he did not convince others to support him. Too many people were dependent upon him, upon the decisions that the lords would make. Scarlett would understand. And she would accompany him now, would she not?

He was just finishing his last piece of correspondence, signing it with a flourish, when there was a slight knock at the door before Abbot's graying head appeared.

"My lord, Lady Oxford has requested all of the staff to gather in the Stone Hall," he said. "I thought that perhaps you may be interested in joining."

"Of course," Hunter said, standing so quickly his chair nearly fell backward, but he caught it just in time. "Ah, Abbot," he said as the man made to leave. "I don't suppose you know what this is all about?"

"I have my suspicions, my lord, but they are just that," said the butler with a smile. "I wouldn't want to be presumptuous."

Hunter narrowed his eyes but nodded, dismissing the man. Just what was his wife up to now?

"I hope you all had a lovely Christmas!" Scarlett was exclaiming as he entered the room, where servants were gathered in the center, some even up on the second-floor balcony as they listened to his wife speak. Goodness, did he really have this many people on his staff? He hadn't thought too much of it before, as he primarily saw to Spicer, Abbot, and Mrs. Shepherd, but he supposed that from the grooms down to the scullery maids, there would be a fair number of them. Did Scarlett know them all?

"And *today*, the day after Christmas, we of course have boxes for all of you!"

Boxes?

"Boxing Day, my lord," Spicer's hushed voice came in his ear. The man could be a spy for how well he was able to sneak up on him. Hunter had heard of the idea, of course, but did anyone actually practice it? His family certainly never had — though, that wasn't saying much as they pretty much skirted anything to do with Christmas. What was his wife up to? And why were all the servants out of their usual dress?

"Mrs. Shepherd and Abbot will help me distribute them," Scarlett continued, and Hunter grinned as he looked at her, finding she had a slight glow about her today, from her wide grin to the animated way she buzzed around like a bee between the pile of boxes sitting beside her and the various members of the staff who approached to help her.

"But before you go, I just wanted to say how much we — ah, here is Lord Oxford now," she waved a hand for him to approach. "How much we appreciate your service, both yesterday through a ... wonderful Christmas, to how much you do for us each and every day of the year. Now, the snow is beginning to clear and the sun is shining. Have a lovely day off, each and every one of you!"

A murmur began to rise from amongst the crowd of them gathered, as Hunter finally made his way to his wife, nodding and smiling at people who approached him with words of thanks.

"Scarlett!" he exclaimed as he finally reached her. "What in heaven's name is happening here?"

"Boxing Day," she said, turning to him with a face full of glee. "Isn't it wonderful?"

"What did you give them?" he asked, slightly concerned as he thought of his pocketbook and his ever-growing donations to charity. He supported it to be sure, but one had to be careful.

"Why, it depends on the person," she said, biting her lip, "doesn't every gift?"

"How did you know what they would enjoy?" he asked, bringing a hand to his head, rubbing his temple.

"Oh, Mrs. Shepherd and Abbot helped," she said, shrugging a shoulder, "but primarily little trinkets or books or something of the sort. Some from our library and items no longer in use, others from the shops in town."

"And the day off?"

"Of course!" she said, looking at him with a bit of chagrin now as she began to sense that perhaps he wasn't as pleased with her actions as she herself was. "That's what Boxing Day is all about."

"Lord Oxford, I must speak with you."

Hunter turned at the dry, gravelly voice, finding the tall man staring down at him. Ah, Stone. He had completely forgotten about the man through all that happened over the Christmas season.

"Mr. Stone," Scarlett said with both greeting and consternation, and the man turned to her, an evil sneer of disgust that even Hunter didn't miss covering his face. "Lady Oxford."

"We best go in my office," Hunter said with a sigh, wishing he could turn back the clock to an hour prior when he had been so pleased with the events of the day. "Come along, Stone."

The man followed him in silence, for Hunter was unsure of what to say to him. He typically left the management of servants to his butler or Stone himself, but he was the only one who could deal with this.

He took a seat behind his desk in his mahogany leather chair, motioning Stone to sit in front of him.

"Your wife has been busy once more," Stone said, looking at him out of his beady dark eyes.

"Yes, I have found that she typically is," Hunter replied,

having no desire to discuss Scarlett with the man with whom she seemed to clash so harshly. "Following our conversation, I spoke with my wife regarding the accounts," he began. "I also visited some of my tenants to determine for myself the true nature of the rents and the spending."

"Oh?" Stone asked, making an apparent attempt to remain unaffected, though Hunter noted his eyes darting from one side of the room to the other in unease, never quite landing on him.

"What happened to the rents, Stone? They were increased so high, my tenants could no longer afford to live in any sort of comfort."

"Tenants were never meant to live in comfort, my lord," Stone said, raising an eyebrow.

"You know what I am referring to, and do not pretend you don't," Hunter ground out, narrowing his eyes at him. "As I don't have the detailed accounts, I have yet to determine where the revenue was placed, but I will soon find out. At any rate, they have now been lowered back to what is appropriate."

"Appropriate according to you, or to your wife?" Stone asked, rising from his chair and placing his hands on the desk. "Are you thinking with your mind, now, my lord, or with what is in your pants?"

"Enough!" Hunter said, rising himself, a finger extended toward his steward. "I will not be shown disrespect, and nor will my wife. You have been with our family for quite some time, Stone, I realize that, but I believe it is time for a change. You are relieved of your duties. Please remove your things from your house by end of day tomorrow."

Stone raised a hand, whether to hit him or simply make his point, Hunter wasn't sure. Reason must have taken hold, however, as he slowly lowered it, simply glowering at

Hunter instead. He pushed back his chair and stormed from the room, though not before pausing as he opened the door.

"You will regret this," he promised, then finally took his leave, and Hunter sank down into his chair, glowering at the man's retreating back.

17

Hunter finally emerged from his study after making a list of all he needed to do before he returned to London, which must, he determined, be in the next few days. Before New Year's, that was for certain, despite how disappointed Lavinia would be at the news.

First, however, he needed a moment alone with his wife, he thought as he strode down the corridor of the hall, which felt empty and hollow in the absence of all of his staff. Finally, he heard voices in one of the far drawing rooms, just beyond the library. Who would she be talking to? Lavinia must have come to visit, he thought ruefully. Ah well, a quick visit with his sister wouldn't be so bad, and then she would be gone by after dinner at the very latest, and they would have utmost privacy. His pulse began to quicken as he imagined all the places they could make love in a completely empty house, without the risk of a servant finding them.

Stone Hall, to be certain. And the library — absolutely the library, where they had first encountered one another upon his return visit. If it was summer, he would have insisted they take things outdoors to the grotto, the jewel of Wintervale, tucked away in his magnificent gardens. That certainly wouldn't do at Christmas, however.

His thoughts came to a halt when he opened the door of the drawing room.

"Hunter!" Scarlett said excitedly as she rose to greet him at the door. "My mother has come to visit!"

"Oh." Hunter stood there in shock, his previous visions of a passionate day and night with his wife evaporating. He knew how much Scarlett loved her mother and was happy she had the opportunity to visit but ... why did it have to be now?

At Scarlett's probing look, he collected himself and entered the room, walking over to the woman, who looked much like Scarlett, but a little older and slightly more ... drawn, he thought. Scarlett had life and vitality — when she chose to share it. Her mother seemed to have given up hope.

"Lady Halifax," he said, bending over her hand. "How lovely to see you again. I apologize that we do not have the proper staff to care for you. We have provided them with a day off for Boxing Day."

"Of course!" she said with a wave of her hand, looking fondly at her daughter, and Hunter could sense the love between the two of them. "I completely understand. I had been worried about Scarlett, you see, as I had thought she was to visit me for Christmas, and with the roads as buried as they were, it wasn't even possible for us to send any correspondence. I was going to write to her, and then I thought, oh Virginia, you are but a few hours away, you might as well go see her yourself."

Lady Halifax smiled at Scarlett, but when she returned

her gaze to Hunter, the edges of it dipped, her pleasure no longer quite making it to her eyes.

"I am surprised to see you here, Lord Oxford."

"I was snowed in as well," he responded, his eyes flicking over to Scarlett to determine her reaction, but her face remained stoic. "Although it has turned out to be fortunate, as it has provided me the opportunity to better get to know my lovely wife."

"I see," Lady Halifax said, nodding her head, looking between the two of them. Scarlett had begun to wind a strand of hair around her finger, chewing her lip as she looked slightly uncomfortable. What was it, exactly, that Lady Halifax saw?

"I believe there is a scullery maid still in the kitchens for the day," Hunter finally said to break the silence. "Why don't I go see if I can have her provide some tea and pastries for you?"

"Very good," said Lady Halifax, apparently finally pleased with him. "I would like that very much."

As Hunter walked out of the room, however, he couldn't help the sense of foreboding that descended upon him. Lady Halifax was a perfectly lovely woman, he told himself. Whatever could be amiss?

"You've fallen in love with him."

"What?"

Scarlett looked at her mother in shock. The three of them had been in the room together for all of five minutes — how could she come to recognize Scarlett's feelings in such a short time?

Virginia Nicholas smiled sadly at her daughter, reaching

over to cup her face in her hands. Scarlett thought, as she always did when she saw her mother, it was like looking into a mirror of her future. The same hazel eyes reflected back toward her, the same freckles over the nose — even her lips were the same shape. But over the years, her mother had developed many lines on her face. Some were from the laughter she and her daughter had shared together, true, but so many were from the dismay she felt upon seeing her husband leave her behind every time he came to visit.

"Oh Scarlett," her mother sighed, stroking her cheek as though she were a young child. "He's a beautiful man to look at, that much is true. But what happened? I thought you were adamant in your decision to keep your distance."

"I was," Scarlett said, choosing her words carefully. "But Mother, over these past few days I have come to know him. He is actually quite ... wonderful. He is considerate, and once he begins to focus on something, he is the most determined man I have ever met."

"When did you marry?"

Scarlett looked at her mother quizzically.

"August, as you well know."

"And how long did it take for him to visit you?'

Scarlett sighed.

"I pushed him away after our wedding. I hadn't expected him to be so ... attractive. And charming, when he puts his mind to it. I was scared by all you had told me. I built up walls around myself so that he couldn't find his way in, couldn't cause me to care for him, to hurt me as Father hurt you. But ... but Mother, not all men are like father."

Her mother began to wring her hands together in her lap.

"I understand that, Scarlett, but look around at the couples of the *ton*. How many are happy — truly happy?

There are far more men with mistresses than there are men without." She tilted her head to the side, a sad expression on her face. "You had to be married, of course, and Lord Oxford seemed as good a man as any. I simply hoped you would understand, would have more sense than I did as a newly married woman. I had so much hope, Scarlett, so much love, and your father ... well, it seemed he did at first too. But then...."

She shook her head sadly, and Scarlett's heart broke at the fluid in her mother's eyes.

"I so badly tried not to love him anymore, Scarlett, truly I did, but I just couldn't help myself. He used that love against me, to keep me with him, to keep me hopeful. Only with age and wisdom did I finally come to understand that it was never to be. I don't want you to have to go through what I did."

Scarlett took both her mother's hands in hers, clasping them tightly as she tried to impart the strength her mother needed so badly.

"I love how much you care for me, Mother, truly I do," she said. "But Hunter ... he loves me, Mother. He told me so."

Virginia's eyes roved over Scarlett's face, and despite the gentleness of her next words, Scarlett could feel the slight rebuke in them.

"When did he tell you this?"

"Last night."

"What were you doing?"

Scarlett's face flushed. She certainly couldn't answer that question, not to her mother. But Virginia smiled ruefully at her, apparently guessing the truth.

"A man will say anything in the throes of passion," she said. "Scarlett, I am not telling you not to be a good wife, not to be with him, or have a family with him. I simply want you to be careful, all right?"

"All right, Mother," Scarlett said in order to appease her. "I will."

HUNTER HAD NEARLY FORGOTTEN about his promise to Lavinia to attend tonight's dinner. Now that Lady Halifax had arrived, however, he was more than anxious to get out of the house. Lady Halifax was polite enough to him, but she looked at him as though he were a fox in a hen house. He had to continually remind himself that he was Scarlett's *husband*, not a blighter out to deflower her and then leave her behind.

Although, he supposed, that was somewhat the truth of their situation. He would prefer not to leave her, but rather wished she would come with him. In fact, that was just what he wanted to speak with her about before they made their way to Nia and Baxter's.

He knocked on the door to her adjoining room. At her call to come in, he cracked open the door, finding her struggling to dress.

"When you gave the staff the day off, did it not occur to you to keep more than a scullery maid in the house for tasks such as these?"

She looked at him with her eyebrows raised, and he chuckled as he walked over to her. "Turn around," he said, tying her stays and then helping her bring the velvet silver gown over her shoulders. For a moment, he thought he should divest her of all her clothing entirely, but they were already running rather late and Lavinia would have his head if he put her off once more.

"Scarlett," he said as he slowly fastened her buttons. "You know I will be returning to London shortly — likely in the next couple of days."

She nodded but said nothing.

"I'd like you to come with me. Please."

Her eyes flew up, meeting his in the mirror. He could sense the panic that registered there, and while he didn't want to push her to do something she so clearly despaired of, he didn't want to think of leaving her behind now.

"No!" she exclaimed, shaking her head wildly. "I will not go to London. I told you this months ago, and again when you arrived."

"Yes," he responded, needing her to understand. "I remember. But I thought things may have changed, that you may have warmed to our ... situation, become more open to the possibilities that may await us there."

She narrowed her eyes. "You mean the possibilities that await *you* there."

"Things have changed," he said, his voice low and husky.

"We have been together one night," she said without emotion. "That doesn't change everything."

"It's more than that, Scarlett," he said, resting his chin on her shoulder as he gazed at her reflection. "I love you. You are my wife, and I want to live that way with you."

"I know," she whispered, though she said nothing else, and his heart rent in two. This was the second time he had told her how he felt for her, and again she stayed silent. He finished buttoning her dress and stepped back from her.

Coldness washed over him, and it had nothing to do with the freezing temperatures outside.

"What's wrong?" he asked, hearing the anger in his voice but unable to keep from allowing his frustration to show. "What have I done to repulse you so?"

"It's not you," she said with a cry, turning around toward him, her silvery gown swishing like moonlight as she did. "I have no wish to return to London. It's where ... it's where..."

"What?" he asked, desperate to know.

"It's where my family fell apart," she whispered, tears gathering in her eyes.

"Talk to me, Scarlett," he pleaded, taking a hesitant step toward her, his hands coming to her arms over the white gloves she had pulled on.

"My parents ... they were happy once," she said, her eyes far away, unfocused. "I used to think how wonderful it was that they loved one another so much when it seemed many other couples care nothing for one another. We followed my father from London to the country, as most do, as you well know. I loved the country — I still do, clearly. I could spend all day with the horses, riding the fields, traveling the countryside. I loved following the neighbor's children around. When we were at our country estate they would spend hours outdoors with me, but then they would go to school once we returned to London. This one summer, when I was ten years old, my mother decided that we could take an extra few weeks at the estate before returning to London. Instead of telling my father when we were to arrive, she thought she would surprise him. We arrived in London later than we anticipated — we got off to a late start, and we stopped to visit a friend on the way. It was just past dinner. We came to the front door, and the butler tried to keep us from entering, but...."

As she told the story, a hand came to her hair, still down upon her shoulders without a lady's maid to attend to it. She worried those strands of hair so much that he wanted to reach out and still her fingers, but he knew if he interrupted, he might never have another opportunity to hear her tale.

"My father was in the drawing room with a woman. Her breasts were practically falling out of her bodice, her skirts hiked up nearly around her waist. My father was hastily trying to rearrange his clothing but ... we knew. My mother went into a fit of hysterics. She had always been under the belief that my father was true to her, that their love was pure. Her eyes were opened that day. When she began to put the pieces together, she realized that never in their marriage had he been without a mistress, never had he been faithful to her. She had been blind to it, not wanting to see it. And even worse, in her mind, was that he took hardly any effort to hide it, allowing this woman into her home — our home."

She paused, her eyes finally focusing on his face.

"I've hated London since then. My mother has hardly ever been able to return to that townhouse, always remembering what she saw there. The worst part of it all, Hunter? My father didn't even care. Oh, he was upset that I witnessed his exhibitions, that's true. But it didn't seem to bother him that my mother knew. And while she never forgot his blatant disregard for her feelings, to this day she continues to love him, despite how much she hates him in equal measure."

Hunter stood there in shock, not knowing what to say. His parents had been cold to one another, had never been loving nor kind toward him. But that was the life he had always known. Scarlett had been part of a loving family — facade that it was — until it had been ripped away from her.

"Scarlett," he finally said, bringing her hand to his lips. "I am so very sorry."

18

W hy had she told him that story?

Her mother's words echoing round her mind, Scarlett had begun to dress this evening determined to put some distance between her and Hunter — not to freeze him out entirely, but to put up some form of protection. Instead, she had shared some of her innermost thoughts with him, making herself even more vulnerable, giving him more power over her.

"Scarlett," he said again, softly, "are you afraid I will do the same to you?"

She wiped at her eyes, dashing the tears away.

"I don't know," she mumbled. "At first, yes. Now ... I am not so sure."

"I wouldn't hurt you like that," he said, his lips tightly pursed. "I could never do that to a woman I love."

"My father told my mother he loved her."

"I'm not sure how to convince you that I am not the same man as your father," he said gently, bringing his index finger and thumb to her chin, tilting her head up to look at him. His blue-green eyes bore into her, as though he were trying to emphasize his point. "But I'm not. Nor am I the same man as my own father. We come from parents who did not set the greatest examples of love for us. But can we not at least try, Scarlett?"

She gave a quick nod. She wanted to try, truly she did. But this had simply been a moment in time, when they were together without the rest of the world's intrusion. What would it be like if she did return to the city with him? She had been in London for only short periods of time over the past ten years. Could she spend months within its confines, as she longed for the freedom the countryside offered her?

Her thoughts continued to plague her as she stepped into the sleigh with her mother and Hunter for the short ride to Lavinia's. This was home now, she thought while they slid away, as she looked up at the impressive brick building, its wings stretching backward to the gardens beyond. She knew nearly every foot of the estate, was familiar with the servants, the tenants. How could she leave all of that behind?

When she turned her face from the view beside her, she saw Hunter looking at her with some concern, and she managed a small smile for both him and her mother.

When they reached the home of the Lavinia and Baxter Shaw, Hunter squeezed her hand as he helped both Scarlett and her mother out of the sleigh. Lavinia was, as always, extremely pleased to see them.

"Oh, and Lady Halifax, how lovely to have you with us!" she said as she led them through the foyer and down the corridor. Scarlett noted that all of Lavinia's servants were still in attendance. Was *she* in the minority of those who celebrated Boxing Day? Surely not. It must simply be Hunter and his sister. "We are a small party this evening. In addition to the four of us, Lord and Lady Raymond are here tonight instead of last night, as they were unable to travel on the roads."

She swung open the door of the drawing room, to reveal Baxter lounging in his usual chair, a mahogany and leather library chair that was completely out of place within the delicate room. Scarlett knew it was rather well worn in the middle — she sometimes wondered if the piece of furniture was part of him. He had a glass of amber liquid in one hand, an unlit cheroot dangling from his lips. She didn't understand what Lavinia saw in the man, but she actually seemed to enjoy his company, so Scarlett didn't question it. As long as Nia was happy, who was Scarlett to judge?

Across from him sat a couple on the chesterfield, a tall, thin man with an easy smile, and a blonde curvaceous woman in a beautiful pink gown. Scarlett had met them at the church in the village before, but had never taken the time to come to know them better. Hunter, apparently, was already on much more familiar terms.

"Madeline!" he exclaimed as the woman rushed toward him, flinging her arms around him. Scarlett felt her heart flip in her chest, as jealousy unlike any she had ever felt before beginning to seep through her veins.

"Oh, Hunter, it is so wonderful to see you!" Lady Raymond said. "It has been ages. Why, I don't think we have had occasion to see one another since shortly after your wedding!"

Which was more recent than the last time Scarlett herself had seen her husband. She caught her mother's pointed stare and raised eyebrow, and she turned her head quickly, doing what she could to prevent her from getting into her head.

"Lady Raymond, Lord Raymond," she said, inclining her head as she swallowed the envy and attempted to be polite.

"How lovely to see you again. This is my mother, Lady Halifax."

"Oh, wonderful to meet you!" said Madeline, releasing Hunter and coming over to the pair of them. "And Lady Oxford, how delightful you look tonight, as you always do."

"And you as well," Scarlett replied, allowing Lord Raymond to take her hand and bow low over it. "Happy Christmas."

"Happy Christmas to all," said Lavinia, sweeping into the room. "This will be such fun, will it not?"

Scarlett wasn't so sure.

DINNER SEEMED INTERMINABLY LONG. Somehow, Scarlett found herself seated at nearly the opposite end of the table from Hunter. It wasn't an overly large table, to be sure, with just the seven of them, but even so, Lady Raymond was seated right next to him, looking particularly thrilled about it.

Scarlett knew she was being ridiculous. The woman was nothing but pleasant and charming, and was simply excited to see an old friend again.

"Oh, and then," Lady Raymond said, continuing the story she was telling about one dance or another that had taken place in a London ballroom, "Hunter brought me a glass of lemonade, but purposely tripped and spilled it all over the vile Lord Vale! How fortunate I was that he was there to free me from the man's clutches. I couldn't have borne one more moment with him breathing all over my face!"

Scarlett tried to force a laugh along with the rest of them, but it was becoming more difficult the more Lady

Raymond spoke. The worst part of it all was that she knew she might actually like the woman, were not all of her stories of Hunter. They had all grown up together, it seemed, their families having been close both in their relationship as well as proximity.

Lavinia and Lady Raymond had been the best of friends since they were girls. But there was something about the way that Lady Raymond looked at Hunter....

"I do hope you will be returning to London as well this Season, Lady Oxford?"

It took a moment for Scarlett to realize that Lord Raymond was speaking to her. She had been so engrossed in the conversation at the other end of the table that she had neglected her own dinner companions, and guilt washed over her.

"I haven't yet decided," Scarlett responded. "Perhaps for a brief time."

"I *do* hope you will," he said meaningfully, and Scarlett's heart began to beat rather rapidly. Was he trying to tell her something, or was she simply being foolish?

"Lady Oxford hates London," Baxter drawled, his first words throughout the entire meal, and his wife backed up his words with a nod.

"Oh yes, London is not for our Scarlett," she said with a smile of affection for her sister-in-law. "Though I have been encouraging her mightily to return with us come February. Baxter and I choose to remain in the country until well after New Year's, but of course, Hunter is so busy with his work that he will be returning shortly. In fact, we are fortunate he is here with us at all — we have to thank the weather for *that*, if nothing else!"

"Oh yes!" said Lady Raymond, placing a hand on

Hunter's shoulder. "Your work is so admirable, Hunter, truly. Tell me more of it?"

"There's, ah, nothing to tell, really," Hunter said, discomfort crossing his face as he frowned slightly. Was he dismissing Lady Raymond, or was he simply annoyed that she was so openly flirting with him in front of the rest of them? At least, Scarlett felt she was. Perhaps she was reading too much into it. But from the look her mother sent toward her from across the table, Scarlett knew that she was also picking up the same sort of intention, though her mother, of course, was always overly suspicious.

Relief descended upon Scarlett when the ladies finally retired to the drawing room. As she rounded the table, eyeing Hunter beginning to light his cheroot, he reached out a hand to take hers, giving it a gentle squeeze and bestowing upon her a small smile before she continued on her way. It was so quick she wasn't sure anyone else noticed, but warmth began to spread through her chest at the fact that he had taken a moment to show her that he did appreciate her — that he was thinking of her, despite Lady Raymond's attempts at stealing all of his attention.

She couldn't help her returned smile, though she felt her mother's hand on her back, urging her into the next room.

Scarlett chose a seat on the rose-patterned upholstery of the settee but had to stifle a groan when Lady Raymond settled in beside her, her pink skirts floating prettily around her ankles.

"Oh, heavens, I ate far too much," the woman said with a laugh. "I keep telling myself I must stop, or I will soon be much too round, but then dinner is set in front of me and I just can't help myself! How I long for a figure like yours, Lady Oxford."

Lady Raymond smiled at her and shame began to work its way into Scarlett's stomach, as she wondered if perhaps she had read too much into Lady Raymond's former actions. The woman had been nothing but kind to her and perhaps she was just being friendly with Hunter, catching up with an old acquaintance. Scarlett was simply being the jealous wife, schooled from years of her mother's own doubts and suspicions.

"And I would love to have curves such as yours," Scarlett responded truthfully as she regarded her own average height, average size, slightly too-small breasts.

Lady Raymond smiled at her conspiratorially.

"You are a lucky woman, Lady Oxford," she said, her voice just above a whisper.

"Oh?"

"Your husband is the most wonderful man I know," she said with a wistful sigh, and then giggled at Scarlett's raised eyebrows. "Oh, I know I shouldn't say such things. Jeremy is a nice enough man to be sure, but when we were younger, I had always hoped that Hunter would see me as more than the friend of his little sister. I took a long time for me to grow into a woman, you see. It wasn't until after I was married to Jeremy that I convinced myself it was time that I show Hunter just how *womanly* I could be, if you know what I am saying. You don't mind me telling you these things, I hope? It's just that from your own disregard for your husband and your preference to spend most of your time apart, I am under the assumption that yours was more of an … arrangement. Not that there's anything wrong with that."

Lady Raymond leaned back, the smile still on her face, her eyes crinkling in the corners as though they were young girls sharing secrets. Only that wasn't the case at all. This woman was speaking of Scarlett's husband as though he were nothing more than a toy to be shared, to be preferred by one woman over another. How dare she? Anger grew in Scarlett's belly, burning so hot that when she tried to speak it came out as a sputter.

"I— Lady Raymond, I think— that is not—"

"Oh, I've shocked you. I'm so sorry. I know that I should be better. Jeremy is always telling me that I need to watch my words. I do, but it's just the two of us now and we understand one another, I believe."

"We do *not* understand one another," Scarlett hissed. "You are speaking of my *husband*, Lady Raymond, and I will not be part of this conversation one moment longer. You have insulted me and my marriage, and I will not have it. Please keep your distance from the two of us."

"Scarlett?" Lavinia came wandering over to the two of them, a look of concern on her face. "Is anything the matter?"

"Nothing to be concerned of, Nia," she said, not wanting to embroil Hunter's sister in a conflict that involved her friend. Scarlett stood and sat down at the pianoforte instead. She wasn't proficient, but she would do anything to get away from Lady Raymond and her vile words. "Nothing at all."

19

Scarlett was unusually quiet on the sleigh ride home. Hunter only wished he could ask her whatever was the matter, but with her mother sitting next to them, he knew he couldn't trust that she would be completely open and honest, and so instead he closed his eyes and leaned his head back, taking a moment to rest on the short ride home, tired from his lack of sleep the night before. The thought made him smile, and he looked forward to the night to come.

Well, hopefully, he thought, opening an eye to look at his wife, who was gazing out at the passing landscape. Her freckled nose was slightly wrinkled, her brow furrowed, and he wondered what it was she was thinking about.

When they returned to the house, he didn't give her a moment alone to begin brooding over whatever was bothering her. He hadn't known her long, but he had come to realize that Scarlett had a tendency to work things over in her mind until she made them into something much more than they were, which could only lead to all sorts of misconceptions.

He followed Scarlett's silvery gown through Stone Hall. The light of the moon filtering in through the windows and shined off the fabric, and she looked as though she was an elfin princess among the boughs and holly lining the room. She was nearly to the stairs when he reached out and caught her against him.

"Hunter?" she asked, looking up at him in surprise. "Is something the matter?"

"You're being careless," he said, looking down at her. "You walked right under the mistletoe and didn't even notice."

He didn't give her a moment to think, but brought his head down, his lips coming to hers, kissing her softly, gently, showing her that his feelings toward her were more than just passion — that he loved her and wanted her to be with him, to show him the same expression back.

While she had never said as much to him, he could feel the returning pressure of her lips, and it gave him hope — hope that she would remain with him, would no longer turn him away.

Hunter broke the kiss, and placed a hand at her back, leading her through the corridor to her bedchamber. He didn't leave her there, however — he followed her in, and when she turned and noticed that he wasn't leaving, she sat down on the edge of the bed while he stoked the fire in the grate. Apparently, the servants hadn't yet returned to their duties, for the room had a chill to it. He noted Scarlett pulling her shawl tighter around her shoulders, and he wanted to go to her, to warm her in ways that would be much more entertaining, but first, he needed this moment to have a frank conversation.

"Scarlett," he said, sitting down in the chair next to the fire, "would you like to tell me what is bothering you?"

She looked from one side to the other, until she finally met his gaze with a sigh. She crossed her arms over her chest.

"Lady Raymond."

"Madeline?" he asked. He wasn't entirely surprised. Madeline had been slightly overeager in her attentions toward him, but he had known her his entire life, as she had been one of Lavinia's best friends since childhood. Her flirtatiousness at dinner was nothing new; it was just how she was. She had always had a bit of a tendre for him, but that was just the remains of girlish infatuation. Though, if Scarlett cared so much, did that mean that she felt something toward him? Hope began to build anew.

"Yes, *Madeline*," she repeated, flinging her name back at him. "Hunter, have you … that is … have you and Lady Raymond ever … been together?"

"Been together? With Madeline? You mean, in a physical sense?" His eyes widened in shock and he couldn't help but chuckle. "Absolutely not! She's … she's Madeline. She's like a sister. Nia's friend. Don't tell me you are jealous."

Scarlett began to play with her hair. "No, of course not," she said, but her face told a different story. "She said some things to me, however, that made me believe otherwise."

"Oh?"

"She told me that she has always been interested in you, but only recently showed you her *womanly* ways. And that she had no problems in saying such things to *me* because our marriage was simply an arrangement and we care nothing for one another."

Incredulity coursed through him. Would Madeline really say such things? But seeing how distraught Scarlett was, knowing that she wouldn't fabricate such a thing, made him believe otherwise. What reason would she have to create such a lie?

"I'm sorry that she said such things to you," he said gently, reaching out and taking her hand in his. "But no, Scarlett, I have never even thought of Madeline in such a sense. She is nearly as much sister to me as Lavinia herself. As to our own marriage — no one has any business speaking of it, though until this past week, I suppose that what she said is correct. But no longer."

He reached up, cupping her chin between his index finger and thumb. "Now, come here, wife. We have some business to attend to."

She smiled at him tremulously. "I'm sorry," she said, shaking her head as she bit her lip. "I shouldn't have doubted you."

"No, you shouldn't have," he said, pulling her to her feet as he threaded his fingers into her hair. "Since I married you, Scarlett, I have been faithful to you, I promise you that, despite the fact that you have wanted nothing to do with me."

"Truly?" she asked, her eyes watering ever so slightly. "All those months alone?"

He smiled ruefully. "I wouldn't say they were an *easy* three months. But I always told myself that when I did marry, I would give it my very best, and, well, had I been unfaithful to you from the beginning, that wouldn't have set us off on a good start, would it have now?"

"No," she said, shaking her head. "Not at all. You have been a good husband to me, despite how horrible I have been to you."

"I wouldn't necessarily say that," he said, dipping his head. "I should have come to you sooner. I was too wrapped up in my work. I didn't put any effort into what we had."

"I didn't give you much reason to."

"I never much believed in what you call the Christmas spirit," he mused. "But I think I've been convinced now that miracles do happen."

"Christmas spirit isn't about what's around you," she said, looking up at him, her eyes shining. "It's from within."

He kissed her then, taking her lips with his, drawing her flush against him. He hungered for her in a way he could hardly explain. No other woman had ever called to him like this before. He didn't know if it was because she was his, or if it was Scarlett herself who made his blood pound through his veins, but he was desperate. He had been so long without her — or any woman — and now he couldn't get enough.

He picked her up, placing her on the bed, and began undressing her as though he were unwrapping a package. He began softly, delicately, but was soon removing her clothes in a frenzy. When he finally had her completely bare, he took a moment to appreciate the true beauty that lay below him before he undressed. Hunter tried to go slow, to take his time, but she hauled him to her before he could do anything further, and with a few quick movements they were gasping, groaning, and finally finding fulfillment with one another.

It was glorious. As he lay there afterward with his wife sleeping in his arms, he never wanted to be apart from her again.

HUNTER SHOULD HAVE LEFT by now, Scarlett mused a couple of days later. The roads to London were clear, and the weather, while freezing, had held. Though she wondered exactly *why* he needed to leave so soon. He spent a good deal of time sequestered in his office, and now she wandered down the hall from her bedroom, knocking on the door before poking her head in.

"Hunter?"

He looked up from his papers. For a moment, his gaze was hazy, unreadable, but soon enough he came back to the moment, grinning as he saw what — or whom — his interruption was.

"I'm sorry, I can come back later," she said, taking a step backward.

"No, no," he said, beckoning her in. "You are always a pleasant interruption."

She walked into the room, running her fingers along his huge mahogany desk. The furniture in here was solid, the walls filled with portraits of previous earls. His father was the marquess, as he would be one day, but he was proud of this seat, which had become part of his family a few generations earlier.

"Do you look forward to becoming the marquess one day?" she asked suddenly, the question falling to her mind, as she realized that her own role would change then too. No longer would she be the mistress of this one home, which had become so familiar to her.

His grin faltered slightly. "No, not overly," he said, leaning back in his chair as he contemplated her. "As you have seen, I am not particularly adept at running even one estate. I have no wish to oversee multiple properties. It means less time away from my duties in London."

She nodded, knowing better than any that what they wanted didn't so much matter, as what would come, would come.

"Something on your mind?" he asked.

"Well, since you speak of London..." she said, finally turning from the back wall and sitting in front of him. "I was wondering when you plan to return. Do you ... do you really have to?"

He frowned, running a hand through his hair, making it stand on end.

"We do not return to actual Session until the first of March," he said, swirling his quill pen between his fingers. "But as you know, the truce papers were signed shortly before we left for our recess. I'm concerned about the outcome, it is true, and prefer to be involved in further decision. We think they are true papers, but one never knows for certain unless you are in the room when they are signed. Besides all that, there are matters that may not seem of great importance to most, but that matter to me. The child mills, the prisons, the asylums. I must garner support for them in order to try to create change. These things take time, and I need other lords on my side."

She nodded. She agreed with him, as much as her heart was telling her otherwise.

It would also mean returning to London, to society. Did she want that? She could hardly handle one barbed comment from Lady Raymond. If she were to return to London for the season, those situations would be rampant. Could she do it?

"I admire what you are doing," she said carefully, not wanting to promise anything.

"Very good," he said with a nod. "Nia has been pestering me about attending her New Year's ball. I'll stay until that is over and then return to London, at least for a time. You are more than welcome to return with me, you know that. In fact, I would very much love you to."

She nodded but refused to commit to anything, though

she appreciated the fact that he was allowing her to make the decision.

"My mother said she will be returning home shortly," she said, and while he tried to hide his relief, she saw it cross his face nonetheless. "I thought you'd be pleased," she added, unable to keep the ire from her tone.

"Your mother is wonderful," he said, and when she raised an eyebrow, he continued. "Really, she is. It's just that … she does not seem to be particularly fond of me."

"My mother worries about me," Scarlett said with a sigh. "She is concerned that you'll leave me, as my father left her."

"I will never do that," he promised her. "Now—"

"My lord?" Abbot interrupted him, and at Hunter's look of consternation, he continued hurriedly. "My apologies, my lord, truly, but—"

"But I would not wait and therefore your faithful butler felt it best that he hurry on ahead of me to warn you."

Scarlett gasped at the cold voice at the door, turning to see Hunter's father enter. He had a similar look to Hunter, but where Hunter was warm and affable, the marquess was cold and calculating. The smile he gave Scarlett made her shiver. She had hardly spent any time in the man's acquaintance — simply the morning of their wedding. Her father had conducted the other necessary arrangements.

"Lady Oxford," he said. "How lovely to see you. And the two of you together. When I heard word that my son was spending more than a week outside of London, I knew there was something that must have been keeping him here. Attempting an heir, are you?"

Scarlett gasped at his forwardness, looking at Hunter, who rose and came around his desk, standing in front of her as though he was protecting her against his father. She knew Hunter respected him and had worked hard to live up to his expectations, so she was shocked at the marquess' rudeness toward her.

"Father. What are you doing here?"

"Wonderful to see you as well, Hunter. Your mother and I decided that we wanted to see our children at Christmastide."

"You both hate Christmastide."

"Yes, well." He shrugged. "Here we are. Lady Oxford, a moment alone with my son, if you please?"

"Would you mind providing us with a moment or two, Father? Scarlett and I were conducting some business, I suppose you could say. I will speak with you directly afterward."

"Business? With your wife?" He raised an eyebrow at his son. "Very well. I will have to go join the ladies."

Scarlett shot up immediately, his words bringing her to the sudden realization that her mother was alone with Lady Rockingham. From what she knew, Hunter's parents were not exactly the warmest people. A barb from his mother could completely undo her own mother, who did not have a particularly strong countenance.

"It's fine," she said, standing, placing a hand on Hunter's arm. "I will leave the two of you. I'll see you at dinner, Hunter."

She began to walk out of the room but her husband caught her fingers, pulling her back toward him, placing a kiss on her lips before he turned to look at his father, as though he had to prove to the man that their bond was one that was more than one forced upon them by their parents. Lord Rockingham smirked.

Scarlett shivered.

20

"Do you think it's a bit much?"

Scarlett twirled in front of the mirror, the skirts of her gold dress with its silver trimming shimmering in the candlelight as she did so. Marion's eyes widened as she watched her.

"Not at all," she breathed. "You are glorious."

Scarlett laughed. "Oh, don't be silly. It's not me — simply the workings of a clever seamstress and expensive, beautiful material. Now, tell me, do you have any plans for this evening?"

She grinned when Marion blushed, beginning to fiddle with the stiff black fabric of her dress.

"We're to have a dance ourselves, downstairs, nothing too elaborate," she said with a wave of her hand. "Though Rupert will be there of course, and oh, my lady, I have never met another like him before!"

"I take it all is progressing well, then?"

"I should say so," Marion said before pausing. "Well, it *was*, although yesterday..."

"What happened yesterday?"

"Lord and Lady Rockingham arrived. Lady Rockingham's maid is a comely one, she is. Rupert's eyes looked as though they would fall right out of his head when she walked into the servant's dining hall. And she was fairly high upon herself, I'll tell you, being the lady's maid of a marchioness and all."

It seemed Marion was just as eager for Hunter's parents to leave as Scarlett was herself. It was a wonder that both Hunter and Lavinia had turned out to be as warm and loving as they were. While Scarlett was pleased that Lord and Lady Rockingham had barely deigned to say more than a few words to her since they had arrived, it was difficult to watch the way they also practically ignored their own children. Hunter seemed resolved to the fact and went about his business, but Scarlett could see the crestfallen expression on Nia's face when her mother had greeted her with a cold kiss, speaking to her only of the gossip of the day.

"They will be gone tomorrow, Marion, not to worry," she said, sitting on the round stool in front of her vanity, kicking her foot on the floor so that she swirled around to face Marion, who now sat on the bed. "Besides that, I'm sure Spicer knows by now what a wonderful woman you are, and how lucky he is to have your affection."

"I hope so, my lady," Marion said glumly.

"Now," Scarlett said, rising and striding over to her wardrobe. "What were you planning to wear for the dance?"

"My Sunday dress, as always."

Scarlett looked over her shoulder at Marion, the grin returned to her face.

"Not tonight."

She rustled through her assortment of dresses, finally finding an evening dress that would suit Marion's coloring, allowing her to stand out while not being too extravagant. "You must wear this."

"Oh, my lady." Despite having dressed Scarlett in the garment many times over, Marion now looked at the fabric reverently. "I could never..."

"Of course you can!" Scarlett encouraged. "Pink suits you, and it is not overly elaborate. You will attract some attention, true, but just enough. It's perfect."

"Thank you," Marion said, beaming at her. "I appreciate it more than you know. Oh, my lady, I wish..."

"Yes?"

"I wish you all the happiness in the world," she said in a burst of emotion. "You've always been so wonderful to me, and I just hope that you and Lord Oxford truly find your love for one another so that you can be together as you were meant to be."

Marion had barely spoken the words when she clapped her hand over her mouth. "My apologies, my lady, I should never have said that."

Scarlett chuckled as she laid the gown on the bed. "It's fine, Marion, and I appreciate your best wishes. We shall see what comes. Anyway, it should be an interesting evening, with both my mother as well as Hunter's parents present at Lavinia's party. What I need now is a spot of luck."

"Good luck, my lady," said Marion, gathering the pink gown in her arms. "And happy New Year."

When Scarlett descended the stairs and rounded the corner, she was surprised to find the first drawing room empty. She peeked into the second drawing room, her gaze catching on Lord and Lady Rockingham. Oh dear. Had they seen her? Perhaps she could sneak— blast. Yes. Yes, they had caught sight of her. Scarlett sighed but forced her feet into the room, walking over to the chair across from them.

"Good evening," she greeted them. Lady Rockingham nodded, while Lord Rockingham simply stared at her. Slightly disconcerted, Scarlett looked down at her hands before returning her gaze to them. While they didn't speak to her, they seemed as though they were ignoring one another as well. Goodness, when was Hunter going to arrive?

"We are so pleased to have you visit us," Scarlett said, forcing a smile to her face.

"This is my home, is it not?" Lord Rockingham said dryly, and Scarlett frowned but swallowed the words that threatened to emerge in retaliation.

"I suppose it is," she responded as politely as she could, though she nearly choked on the phrase. "Have you seen my father recently?"

She knew the marquess was friends with her father, or an acquaintance at any rate. Apparently, she had asked the wrong question, however, for a look of undisguised rage cross the marquess' face.

"No, he has not seen your father," the marchioness said, finally speaking. She tossed a smirk at her husband. "But I have."

Scarlett looked at her, puzzled. Why would the marchioness have seen him and not the marquess? Did they not run in the same social circles? And why was the marquess so angry— oh. Oh no. She couldn't mean ... but, apparently she did. Lady Rockingham smiled at Scarlett's look of incredulity.

"Your father is an ... old friend of mine as well," she said, taking a sip of the deep blood red wine in her hand. "Isn't that right, Spencer? Lord Rockingham has only recently realized this, my dear. Now, Scarlett, I am pleased that you are spending time with my son. You will be returning to

London soon, will you not? You can hardly remain ensconced away alone in this horrid estate by yourself. Why, what will people say if you continue to send your husband off to London alone? It is also quite important that you beget an heir rather soon. It was why you married, was it not?"

"There's not much else a wife is good for," Lord Rockingham ground out, sending a glare his wife's way.

"Excuse me?" Scarlett finally exclaimed, and both of them turned to look at her in shock.

"While I am much more inclined to say what is on my mind than the average lady, this is beyond acceptable. Why, my mother could walk into the room at any moment, and I would highly prefer she not listen to this nonsense you speak."

"Your mother always was the delicate sort," Lady Rockingham said with a sniff, and Scarlett threw up her hands.

"Hunter loves and respects the both of you," she said in a low voice. "Be the parents he requires."

"Are you finished?" Lady Rockingham asked, an eyebrow raised.

Scarlett actually had much more to say, but when she opened up her mouth to retort, she heard footsteps entering the room.

"Good evening," her mother said softly from her place in the doorway on Hunter's arm. "How lovely you all look tonight. Happy New Year."

"Happy New Year, Mother," Scarlett said, walking over and embracing her before casting a warning look at Lady Rockingham, who frostily ignored her.

"Scarlett, you look..." Hunter's voice trailed off as his eyes began at her face, leaving a trail of fire as though he were running his hands over her. His perusal continued down to pause at her bosom, then traveled the expanses of her shimmering skirts, before his eyes finally returned to her face. He winked at her, which didn't go unnoticed by the pair in the corner as Scarlett heard Lady Rockingham snort.

As they were already late as it was, they had no time for a drink but began to make their way outside to the carriage. As they did, Lady Rockingham affixed herself to Scarlett's side.

"Enjoy the infatuation he currently holds for you," she whispered. "It does not last long."

And with that she was striding down the hall ahead of the rest of them, her head held regally high, Scarlett watching her with narrowed eyes all the way.

LAVINIA HAD OUTDONE HERSELF, creating a New Year's party unlike anything Scarlett had ever seen before. While her home with Baxter was not nearly as large as Wintervale, she had an eye for beauty. And though the Tannon family had never recognized the Christmas season, they had always been sure to attend — or host — a New Year's celebration. All attendees came in their best, and Lord and Lady Rockingham were never ones to shy away from showcasing their very finest.

And fine everyone was tonight. A couple dozen people were gathered in the ballroom, many having traveled a fair distance to be here tonight. Thankfully, the weather had held, the winds continuing from the south — which spoke of warm tidings for the year ahead, if Hunter recalled the phrase correctly. He could only hope, after the freezing winter they had endured so far.

None in attendance, however, were as lovely nor as fair

as his wife. She shone brighter than any star above, and he noted a fair number of heads swinging toward them as they entered the ballroom. Lavinia fairly bounded up to them, welcoming them and urging them into the room. Baxter nodded at them, drink in hand and yet another unlit cheroot dangling from his lip.

It had been some time since Hunter had attended an event in the area, though he had seen many of the *ton* in London. Apparently, he and Scarlett — particularly together — were a novelty. It didn't take long for him to be surrounded by men questioning him about the peace signings just prior to the Christmastide recess, and Scarlett excused herself with a smile, nodding to him before going off to join Lavinia, who was thrilled to introduce Scarlett to many of her friends who were not from the area.

Interestingly, Lavinia scarcely acknowledged her parents, who stood looking out over the ballroom, disdain apparent in their turned-up noses and cool glances which they passed around the room. When Lavinia did glance their way, Scarlett could read the hurt in her gaze, and she was determined to be as good of a friend — and sister-in-law — to Lavinia as she could. She also felt that it was time someone told them exactly of the consternation they were causing their children. When Scarlett saw her mother join the two of them, she decided she should join the conversation herself.

"What a lovely home your daughter has," her mother was saying to the marquess and marchioness.

"It is well enough, I suppose," said Lady Rockingham. "Why she insisted on marrying Baxter Shaw I will never know. A viscount is well enough but the man—"

"Loves Lavinia," finished Scarlett. She didn't care overly much for Baxter herself, but he did love Lavinia. They should be glad their daughter found herself in a happy marriage.

"Yes, well," sniffed Lady Rockingham. "Love can only take one so far."

It was one point Lady Halifax seemed to be in agreement upon, for she slowly nodded her head, a sad smile on her face.

"Hunter and Lavinia are pleased to have you here for the New Year's celebration," said Scarlett. "They have missed you."

Lord Rockingham snorted as though speaking of such emotions was below him, while Lady Rockingham frowned at her. "They both found their place in life," she said. "They no longer need their parents."

"One always appreciates his or her parents," Scarlett said, looking to her own mother, wondering what it would be like to live without her love. Even her father, whom she resented for his treatment of her mother, still loved her in his own way, and she never doubted that he would provide her with anything she might need, were she to only ask for it.

"Oh, don't be so base," Lady Rockingham said. "That is what nursemaids and governesses are for — children."

Sorrow filled Scarlett's breast at the thought of Hunter and Lavinia as children, ignored by their parents. She pictured them as they waited, every Christmas, for the gift of acknowledgment, with none ever coming. At the very least, they had always had one another.

"Ah, Madeline Lancaster is here," said Lady Rockingham, changing the subject, a slow smile crossing her face. "Although of course she is, given that she and Lavinia have always been such good friends."

"Yes, we met them the other night," Lady Halifax said, offering no further information.

"I had always thought that she and Hunter ... ah well, never mind," said Lady Rockingham, turning an icy smile on Scarlett. "She chose to marry Jeremy Lancaster before Hunter was ready to marry himself, so we should no longer speak of it, should we?"

"She and Hunter are, in fact, on the dance floor at this very moment," added Lord Rockingham, finally joining the conversation.

"Ah, so they are," Lady Rockingham said with a smirk and a gleam in her eye when she looked at Scarlett. "They do look well together, do they not?"

Scarlett had tried to make peace with Hunter's parents — she truly had. But she couldn't take another moment of conversation with them. She took her mother's arm in her own and steered her across the room. She could feel her mother's eyes on her, but she didn't want to speak to her of Hunter and the beautiful Lady Raymond. Hunter had told her that he was faithful and always would be, and she believed him. But that didn't alter how much it hurt to see him laugh and flirt with another woman. Was this what she would be reduced to if she followed him to London? Watching from the sidelines while he lived his life as a treasured member of the *ton*?

She reached up a hand to tug at a curl, winding it around her fingers, as she couldn't help but watch the two of them go around the ballroom. What was she to do?

"Be careful, Scarlett," was all her mother said from beside her, as she laid a hand on her arm. "Please, darling ... just be careful."

21

Mercifully, all of their parents left early on New Year's Day.

They had stayed at Lavinia's until well into the first day of 1814. Hunter had found his wife in time for a kiss as the clock chimed midnight, though her kiss didn't seem quite as urgent as usual. She seemed ... distracted, though it was likely due to the many other guests nearby. He had also seen her talking with his parents earlier, which was always a recipe for disaster. He had been eager to take her home and celebrate in a much more private way with just the two of them.

This morning, in the light of day shining in through the window, he closed his eyes to recall her shimmering silver gown, so lovely on Scarlett, though he much preferred when it became a pool of fabric on the floor of his bedchamber. He had appreciated the glow of Scarlett's pale skin, illuminated by the fire in the grate, even more than the lovely dress that so many at the party had commented on.

He was a lucky man, he had thought as he had fallen asleep the night before. A very lucky man indeed.

And now the house held only the two of them, alone together at last. He grinned as he rose from the bed after Scarlett scurried out of the room through the adjoining door to her own chambers, just as Spicer entered from the corridor.

"Good morning, my lord!" the man boomed, and Hunter brought a hand to his head. He had indulged in a few spirits the night before, and now Spicer seemed altogether too cheery.

"Happy New Year, Spicer," he murmured, and his valet responded in kind.

"You seem ... overly pleased this morning."

"That I am, my lord, that I am," Spicer responded. "All of my wishes for this upcoming year came true within the first few hours. I am to be married, my lord — married!"

"What?" Hunter came alert then, his eyes widening. "To the maid?"

"Marion Parker," Spicer said, his eyes far away as he looked beyond Hunter and out the window. "Although ... I suppose I should have spoken with you about it first, my lord. I know she and I are both in service to you and all..."

"It's fine, Spicer," Hunter said, shaking his head with a grin as he reached out a hand to his valet. "Congratulations."

"Thank you, my lord. Thank you very much!"

And now all Hunter had to do was convince his wife that the two of them belonged together as much as his valet and her maid.

"Oh, my lady, I wish you could have been there!" Marion

was telling Scarlett the same story, though with a bit more detail, just a room away. "Well, not that you would have been to a servant's gathering, of course, but—"

Scarlett held up a hand with a slight chuckle. "I understand your meaning, Marion. Continue, please."

"Well, Lady Rockingham's maid was there, of course, in what she thought, I'm sure, would be the most brilliant gown of all. But then, when I arrived in *your* gown, oh my lady, you should have seen how wide her eyes became! And she was practically hanging off of Rupert's arm, but the moment I walked in, our eyes met, and I swear to you, that was the last either of us looked elsewhere for the entire night. When the New Year arrived, he kissed me, and then he knelt down in front of me and asked me to be his wife — his wife!" Marion's eyes were filled with tears as she came over to Scarlett. "Would that be all right with you, my lady? If I were married, and to another of the staff?"

"Of course," Scarlett assured her, her hands grasping Marion's. "I only want you to be happy, and it sounds as though your Rupert makes you that way."

"Oh, he does," said Marion with a sigh. "He truly does."

"You must know, however..." Scarlett trailed off, her gaze out the window at the snow-covered trees. "You may have to choose, Marion. I do not want to lose you as my lady's maid, I truly don't, but if I remain in the country while Lord Oxford is in London, if you stay with me, you may go months at a time without your husband. I'm sure we can find another position for you if you prefer, so that you can accompany him."

Marion's mouth opened slightly in surprise. "But my lady, I thought..."

She trailed off at Scarlett's expression.

"I will wait for your decision," she murmured, and Scarlett nodded, turning her head before her maid noticed that tears were beginning to fill her eyes. She wanted to remain with Hunter, truly she did, but she was scared — scared of who she would become if she gave her heart fully to him, if she followed him to London, where she would witness the ladies of the *ton* dancing and flirting with her husband as Lady Raymond did the previous night.

She should hardly be jealous. Of course, Hunter danced and spoke with other women, as did all men in polite company, but he always came back to her. While her heart swelled with gratitude to him for it, she didn't want to have to experience the conflicting emotions night in and out, coupled with her hatred of the city. Perhaps it was better to remain here alone, ignorant of all that occurred in London.

She sighed as she dressed in a cheery yellow frock that belied her current mood. For Hunter would be returning shortly, she knew. The question was, would she accompany him or not?

HUNTER SPOKE at length of their London return over breakfast that morning. He could admit that he was being a coward, not asking his wife directly if she deigned to return with him, but he didn't want to hear her refusal, didn't want to think of her rejecting his request. And so, he decided he would simply assume that she would be accompanying him, and surely she would follow along. When she didn't protest any of his ideas, he took that as her agreement.

"Tomorrow morning, then," he said with a nod. "That should work very well, indeed. Lord Falconer will be able to provide me an audience the following day, and we should get to work at determining the best way to go about arranging your charities before I must return to the House of the Lords. We will also be back at Wintervale in a few weeks as I must find a new steward, of course, but luckily we aren't far from London."

Scarlett nodded, and while Hunter could sense her hesitancy, he was sure it was simply some nerves upon returning to London, as it had been some time, he knew, since she had been there.

"Scarlett," he said softly, taking her chin between his index finger and thumb, tilting her head toward him. "I know London holds unpleasant memories for you. But we will be living in our own home, making our own new, happy memories. I will never do to you what your father did, you know that, do you not?"

"I do."

"Then do not fear. If you ever need anything, I will be there for you, you must believe me."

"Of course, Hunter. But..."

"But what?"

"You have your life there already. Your work, your clubs, your friends. I have no wish to be entirely dependent on you."

"You have your own hobbies," he said, frowning. "You will have your charities, and I am sure you will volunteer. You will also have plenty of time for both your friends and your horses as well."

"My horses and my friends are here," she said quietly. "Though I suppose you are right, I shall have my charities, and I do thank you for arranging everything for me."

"Hyde Park can be a wonderful place to ride," he said in what he hoped was a cheerful manner. "And you'll make new friends, you'll see. Lavinia will arrive in London by

March. And people will love you! It will be fine, not to worry, love."

As he took in her look of consternation, however, he realized that he was trying to convince himself as much as her. For she was right. He *was* rather busy in London. This time in the country had been a wonderful respite, and he was grateful for it in so many ways as it had provided him with the opportunity to fall in love with the woman sitting in front of him, the woman who was kind and generous and adventurous and beautiful — and currently silently resenting the fact that she would have to leave the home she had come to know so well. He understood this, but what else could he do? He certainly didn't want to truly leave her. They would make this work.

But that night, as he made love to Scarlett, when she began to tremor around him, finding her release, her arms came encircled him in a grip so tight, tears dripping onto his shoulder, that he couldn't help the fear in his breast as he wondered if she was, in fact, saying goodbye.

SCARLETT STOOD in her room the next morning, looking at the valise in front of her. Hunter wanted to leave by noon, she knew, in order to take advantage of the most light and warmth of the day. The carriage was ready, his bags packed. But the longer she stood there, the faster her heart beat. She wandered over to the window, looking down at the snow-covered grounds below. She knew what he expected of her was nothing untoward, was typical for a married couple, to go where the husband needed to be. And yet everything within her longed to remain. She had come to love the land, the people, the estate. This was home. They would return, true, but it wouldn't be until the snow had melted, the ground had thawed, and the gardens would be blooming once more with the summer sun.

Could she do it? Could she leave all behind for Hunter? She knew, deep in her heart, that she loved him with all of her being, and that scared her more than even simply leaving did. For if she left, her whole world would revolve around him. All of her emotions would be tied up in him, while he would be devoted entirely to other causes and purposes. It was not a life she had ever wanted to live. And yet, here she was.

As Marion puttered around the room, packing all of Scarlett's remaining essentials, Scarlett slowly put one foot in front of her as she walked along the corridor and down the stairs, attempting to quell the panic within her. Her stomach in turmoil, she stood at the threshold between the Oak Room and the entrance hall. She looked up, seeing the mistletoe hanging above her, and tears sprang into her eyes once more.

When she tilted her head back, she found Abbot standing there, looking at her with a gentle smile.

"We didn't remove the Christmas decor," she said sadly. "Typically I wait until Twelfth Night, but..."

"It's all right, my lady, we are happy to do it," he said with a nod of his head. "We will miss you, to be sure, but you are where you belong."

"Oh yes," said Mrs. Shepherd joining him, and the two of them beamed at her as though they were proud parents. "We are so pleased that you and my lord will be together, as it should be."

Scarlett nodded stiffly, and suddenly she felt an arm slip around her. She turned to find her husband standing in front of her, his formal dress covered in a cloak, a fur hat upon his head.

"One last kiss under the mistletoe," he said, dropping a quick smack on her lips. She began to walk through the door he held open for her, but once she was through the entrance hall, her foot on the cusp of the portico, she stopped. She couldn't seem to take one more step, her body frozen as she looked out before her, at the carriage surrounded by the snow, the evergreens a backdrop behind it.

"I can't," she said, the words coming from her lips before she even had time to think of them, nor the consequences.

"What's this?" asked Hunter, his hand coming lightly to her back. "Is everything all right?"

"No," she said, shaking her head. "It's not all right. I want to be with you, Hunter, I do, but … but I can't go back there. Not now, not for months on end. I will see you when you return. I look forward to it, truly, and I have so loved our time together. But I can't go back with you. I'm sorry."

And with that, she turned and ran back the way she came as Hunter called her name.

"Scarlett!" he cried out, his footsteps echoing hers, and finally she stopped in the middle of Green Hall, knowing that she could never outrun him. "Don't do this," he begged, his eyes filled with desperation. "All will be fine, I promise. Just come with me."

"Can you not stay?" she asked, her breast filled with hope. For he wasn't required in London, not truly, for another few months. No, he was simply *choosing* to be there. "At least for a time?"

"I must go back," he said, his voice deep and grave. "Please, Scarlett, won't you come with me? I love you, and I want — I *need* you with me."

"I can't," she whispered, her voice breaking. "I will see you when you return, whenever that may be. I'm sorry."

And with that, she began running once more, her booted feet echoing down the corridor, and she didn't know whether she was relieved or dismayed when he didn't follow her.

22

Scarlett all but ran up the stairs to her bedchamber, slamming the door and sinking down in a crouch against it, until she found herself a blubbering mess on the floor. This wasn't like her, not at all. She was normally assured, confident, willing to take on whatever risks came her way. Her mother had been right. It was love that made her this way. Weak. Inconsistent. Unsure. She had been resolved to go with Hunter to London, until that final moment. Now he would hate her, she was sure of it. Would he find comfort in the arms of someone else? Someone like Lady Raymond? The thought created an ache within her that began in her heart and radiated out through her entire body, her limbs practically trembling with it.

She rocked back and forth from her seat on the floor, her arms around her knees. She didn't know how long she stayed that way until finally there was a soft knock on the door.

"My lady? My lady, are you all right?"

Marion. Oh, God. Scarlett had been so caught up in her own troubles she had completely forgotten Marion. And now Mr. Spicer would be long gone with his master. In running from Hunter, she had effectively kept the two of them from one another.

"Marion!" she cried, opening the door, and the girl practically stumbled in. "Oh, Marion, I'm so sorry. I never thought ... I should have—"

"It's fine," said Marion with a gentle smile. "We will sort it out. I couldn't leave you, not now. Not like this. I'm sorry, my lady, but I couldn't help overhearing your exchange with Lord Oxford. Do you not think you could come to enjoy London? Perhaps in due time? You could even go back and forth between here and the city, could you not?"

"You are likely right, Marion," Scarlett said with a sigh, making her way to the window, her cloak trailing on the floor behind her. The carriage was no longer in sight, long passed into the snowy drifts beyond. "I could, I suppose. I want a life with him, I do, but I fear once we are in London, *our* life will become *his* life. And should anything happen, I will be completely lost."

"Like your mother."

"Like my mother."

"I do not believe Lord Oxford is like your father, if I may be so bold to say, my lady," said Marion hesitantly. "Though only you know that for sure."

"Have I made a mistake?" Scarlett asked, turning from the window, looking beseechingly at her maid.

"That is not for me to say, my lady," murmured Marion. "Just know that I am here for you, whatever you may need."

"Thank you, Marion," Scarlett said with a soft smile.

"Oh, and my lady..." Marion pulled out a package that had been hidden behind her back. "My lord asked me to give this to you."

What in heavens...? Scarlett looked at Marion with some

question as she took the small package wrapped in brown paper. She turned it over in her hands, pulling on the twine that bound it together.

"Whatever could this be?" she murmured, intent on opening it.

"I wouldn't know, my lady," responded Marion. "Would you like me to leave?"

"No, no, stay," Scarlett said as she walked to her vanity, sitting down on the stool in front of it. She finally managed to tear off the remaining packaging, and she pulled out a piece of clothing. As she unfurled the garment, a piece of paper fell out, and as curious as she was of the gift, she needed to know first of the note.

"*Happy Christmas, my love,*" was all it said. And in her hands she held a pair of breeches, looking as though they were tailored exactly to fit her. Tears sprung up anew in her eyes, but this time for another reason entirely. He not only loved her, but he *knew* her. He loved her despite the fact that she rode a horse in the most unladylike fashion possible, and he not only accepted it but he was encouraging it.

"There are words written on the back, my lady," Marion said in a near whisper.

Scarlett picked up the paper she had discarded on the vanity.

"*While this is not a tangible gift, I have set up a foundation for you. You can choose the charities, be they in the village or within London. The funds are available and you may manage it, however you see fit.*"

She blinked. Did he mean it? She knew she had told him of what she wanted, but for him to go ahead, to create something for her, was unbelievable. It would give her purpose, outside of simply a life created around him.

As the tears slid down her cheeks, she thought of how

he had embraced Christmastide, despite the fact that he was not particularly enamored with the holiday. He had shown her with his lovemaking how much he desired her, had stood up for her to his parents, to his friends, staying by her side whenever she needed him.

And all of this after she had been so frosty toward him. And then she left him, unable to overcome her doubts.

She had made a mistake, allowing her fear to overrule all else, even her love for him. She had to make things right, to tell him exactly how she felt.

He had taken the carriage. Surely she could catch him on horseback.

She began to don the breeches, calling out to Marion to find her riding gear.

"I must catch him, Marion. *I must!*"

As THE CARRIAGE trundled down the bumpy road away from Wintervale, Hunter felt like he had left a piece of himself behind. In just over a week, his wife had become as much a part of him as one of his very own limbs. When he returned home, he had hoped they could find a way to come together in a true partnership, but never could he have imagined forging a bond so strong. He had thought she felt the same, had tried to coax the words out of her, but they never came. Had he simply been imagining her response to him? He had told her he loved her time and again, and all he had received in return was a warm smile, a gentle kiss, or tender words that were welcomed but did not return his sentiments.

If she loved him, as he truly needed her to, she would have come with him. But without that love, she had not found the courage to overcome all of her fears. They had

ELLIE ST. CLAIR

failed one another, and now he would never be the same again.

He leaned down, his elbows on his knees, his head in hands. Finally lifting them, he looked out the window at the evergreens passing by. He would never look at greenery the same way, he thought with a rueful grin. Wringing his hands together, he opened his small valise to find the correspondence he needed to review before meeting with Lord Falconer tomorrow. As he pulled out the documents with gloved hands, something fell out of the bag to the floor of the carriage. He was going to leave it there, but a flash of red caught his eye. He picked it up, wonder widening his eyes as he looked at the sprig of holly held in his hand. How had it gotten there?

He twirled it around, surprised at the warmth beginning to grow within him as he thought of the trees outside, the snow swirling against the window of the carriage, and the little red berries encased in greenery which he now palmed. The warmth was Christmas. And Christmas was Scarlett. She had caused him to love the holiday, had made him believe that true love could actually exist between two people. She had rejected him, true, but she had demons of her own, a past that she had shared with him, and he had quit on her too early.

He had pushed, demanding that she return to London with him, never considering that perhaps in order to be together, they must find a compromise. He could never spend all of his time in the country, to be sure, but could he not spend more of it here? And he did not live particularly far from London. Would it truly be that hard to compromise? He had expected her to change her life in order to follow along with his. But he was being too stubborn, too set in his ways. He never should have left, but that didn't mean he couldn't return and bring things to rights.

Hunter banged on the top of the carriage to alert his driver.

"Chaucy! Turn around! We're going home for my wife!"

THE WIND WHIPPED past Scarlett's ears with increasing frigidness. She had been stupid. In her haste to chase after Hunter, she had dressed hurriedly — though warmly — and raced to the stables. There, the surprised groom had helped her prepare her mount, and she had declined his repeated offers to accompany her. Why had she not let him? She berated herself now for her hasty decision. She supposed she had seen herself finding Hunter and proclaiming some romantic declaration, and had considered that it would feel somewhat silly with a groom in tow.

But now the skies, which had been sunny when she devised this hasty plan, were beginning to darken, the winds increasing in strength, the temperature dropping rapidly. She was moving at a quick pace, but would it be quick enough? Her hands were already beginning to stiffen with cold, and she mumbled an apology to Star. By now, she was hopefully closer to Hunter than she was to home, however, so she pushed on.

The path wound around the cliffs next to the river below, but there was one thing she was confident in, and that was the sure-footedness of her horse. As they rounded the path overlooking the frozen lake, however, suddenly Star reared up. Scarlett squeezed tightly with her thighs, but her hands were so cold she couldn't properly grip the reins, and they slipped out of her fingers as she went flying backward. She landed hard on the path behind her, a jolt of pain cracking through her ankle and radiating up through her leg. She gasped from the shock of it, all of the breath knocked out of her body.

She felt tears gather in her eyes as she fought down the panic, finally maintaining a hold on control. There was a pain her chest but she was, at least, able to breathe again.

"Stupid, Star, that's what I am," she mumbled to her horse, who leaned down and nuzzled her ear in support. Why had he spooked? Star was a well-trained animal who had never faltered before.

Scarlett came to all fours, trying to determine just how injured her ankle was. It throbbed painfully, but as long as she could make it onto Star, she would be fine. Scarlett tried to stand, but when she tried to put weight on her ankle, it buckled, not taking any of it.

Grasping onto the stirrup hanging off of Star, Scarlett managed to pull herself to standing on one foot, but it was then she faced a dilemma. She couldn't stand on her left foot in order to put her right in the stirrup, and if she stood on her right to put her left foot in the stirrup, she wouldn't be able to give it any weight to mount. She jumped on one leg, grasping the pommel as she tried to haul herself up, but she only slid back down again, her chest hurting something fierce, her breath still coming in short gasps. Star was too tall, too wide in girth.

Scarlett whimpered at the hopelessness of her situation. No one would be out in a storm like this. No one would find her. She had to determine a way of out of this herself.

Just in case, she sent a cry out, hoping for the impossible — that someone would hear her, could help her out of this predicament she had stupidly found herself in.

"Help! Is anyone there? Please help me!" She called, and

was so shocked she nearly screamed once more when the tree branches began to rustle beside her.

"Hello? Is someone there?"

Her relief turned to dismay, however, at the man that appeared before her as he emerged through the trees.

"Well, well, Lady Oxford," came the smirking voice of Mr. Stone, calling to her in the wind. What was the steward even doing here? They had thought he had left days ago. "Got yourself in a predicament here, have you?"

"Yes," she said weakly. "I don't suppose you could help me onto my horse? I really just need a hand, and then I'm sure I can make it home."

"I'd like to help you," he said, clearly implying the opposite, "but unfortunately I find myself feeling rather *uncharitable* at the moment, being without employ any longer, nor references to find myself another placement. Now I wonder what — or who — caused that?"

"Mr. Stone," Scarlett said desperately, "I realize you are angry, I do. But I could *die* out here if the storm continues."

"And wouldn't that be a pity, you being such a pretty thing?" he sneered, walking over to pet Star's nose. "Too bad you couldn't keep yourself out of my business and live like a usual countess. Your stallion here is a lovely piece of horse-flesh, despite how easily he spooked."

Scarlett's eyes narrowed with the realization that he had purposefully spooked the horse. The bastard. "Leave him be," she commanded.

"Ah, my lady, here's the issue. I no longer have to listen to anything you say! I think I'll be taking him with me. Farewell, my lady! How long do you suppose it will be until the earl finds himself a new bride?"

And with a cackle, he pulled on Star's reins, urging the horse forward. But Star refused to budge. The horse was as stubborn and loyal as she was, and she managed a smile at Stone's curse when Star refused to take even one step forward. Finally, Stone tossed the reins away in disgust. "Keep your horse," he snarled. "He's good for nothing anyway." He turned, his boots crunching away, leaving her completely and utterly alone.

23

————

Hunter was so eager to return home that he became uncharacteristically frustrated when the carriage began to slow as they were about to turn into the drive. "Chaucy! What is the matter, man?" He knew a storm was brewing, but was that not a greater reason to return with all haste? Instead of speeding up, however, the groom slowed the carriage to a stop, and Hunter had the door half open before Chaucy was even down from his bench.

"What in the…"

He quickly saw what the issue was. There was a horse wandering the path ahead of them, a bundle of something tossed over its saddle. As Hunter approached, his heart began to beat wildly as he recognized the horse — it was Star, his wife's prized stallion. What was he doing out here in this weather? Had he run off? But no — he was saddled. That meant—

"Scarlett? Scarlett!?"

He looked from side to side desperately for his wife as

Chaucy walked over to collect Star. Suddenly the driver began shouting urgently.

"My lord! Come quickly!"

"Chaucy, I cannot see to a horse, not when my wife—"

"But my lord, she is here!"

Hunter ran over, seeing as he did, that the bundle of cloth nearly covered by snow, overtop the horse was a person — his wife. She was slumped so low over the horse's neck he had hardly been able to see her form.

"Scarlett!" he shouted, running to her, fear coursing through him at her prostrate body, which looked so frozen, her lips blue when he lifted her off Star, pulling her into his arms as he kneeled in the snow.

"Scarlett, oh Scarlett, what happened? Open your eyes, love, open your eyes!"

At last, she did as he commanded, though her gaze was unfocused, and while her teeth began chattering violently, at least it was better than the stillness of the previous moment.

"What in the hell are you doing out here?" he demanded.

She attempted to answer, but he shook his head to stop her, despite the fact that he had, in fact, asked the question. "Never mind that for now. We must get you warm and into the house as quickly as possible. Chaucy, will you see to the horses?"

At the man's nod, Hunter lifted his wife into the carriage, sitting down himself and holding her close in an attempt to warm her as best he could.

"Hunter," she said weakly, and despite his best attempt to tell her not to speak, she insisted. "Hunter, I must tell you something."

"Yes?"

"I love you."

She lifted her head, her hazel eyes boring into him, as though pleading for him to hear her, to understand. He more than understood. Those three words released emotions within him of an intensity that he had never known was possible, coursing through his body, causing him to tremble nearly as much as she. He felt wetness on his face, which at first he attributed to melting snow, but soon he realized they were tears. He couldn't remember the last time he had cried, but now they dripped down his cheeks faster than the snow that fell from the sky.

"I'm sorry ... I'm sorry I didn't tell you sooner."

"Oh, Scarlett," he said, pulling her close. "Don't be daft. Just stay with me now, here, until we can get you home and warm. I'm the one who should be sorry for leaving you."

Her eyes were closing then, so he did all he could do at the moment, holding her close, rocking, and praying that all would be all right.

SCARLETT FELT heat upon her yet frigidness within when she finally opened her eyes, turning her head back and forth to see the fire burning merrily in the grate to one side of her, her husband sleeping in the chair on the other side.

"Hunter?" she murmured, and he snapped to attention, the wild curls of his hair swirling about his face in even more abandon than usual, his eyes red and tired, his cheeks pale. "Are you all right? Shouldn't you be in London?"

"Scarlett," he said, coming down to kneel beside her. "You're awake."

"Of course I'm awake," she bit her lip. "I'm speaking with you, aren't I?"

He chuckled then, a laugh filled with relief as he placed his forehead against the hand he gripped in his own. "I was so worried about you."

Suddenly her wild ride came flashing back in jolts of memories — her fall, Stone's threats, her attempt to make it home. She must have made it, she thought, though she didn't have any recollection of how she came to be in her bed. But how had Hunter come to be here?

"Why are you here?" she asked with bemusement.

"I'm here for you," he said simply.

"How long has it been since I fell off the horse?" she asked, trying to sit up further, but found her chest still ached when she moved too quickly.

"Since yesterday," he replied, stroking her fingers. "We gave you something to help you sleep and ease the pain."

"Who sent for you? I would have been fine, really. I—"

"No one sent for me," he said, astonishment crossing his face. "You don't remember, then, much of yesterday?"

"I remember falling from my horse, seeing Stone. I remember finally managing to lift myself up on Star. It took forever and it hurt, oh so much. But I knew if I didn't, I could freeze to death out there, and the storm was getting worse. But then I was tired, and cold and ... I don't know, I must have made it home, or I wouldn't be here."

"What do you mean, you saw Stone?" his eyes narrowed, taking on a suspicious gleam.

"Oh Hunter, that man is evil," she said recounting to him the story. By the time she had finished, Hunter was pacing the room, his features hardened into a countenance so grim she would have been scared had she not known him so well.

"I will kill him!" he ground out.

"You can't kill him."

"He will pay." He stopped pacing then, turning to look at her. "Those words ... that's exactly what he said to me — that I would pay for getting rid of him. Apparently, he thought this was the way to make it happen."

Scarlett shook her head in wonderment at how far some people were willing to go to get what they wanted, even if it meant hurting others.

"We mustn't stoop to his level, Hunter," she said. "Tell the appropriate authorities and hopefully they can find him and punish him accordingly. Promise me?"

After a few moments, he nodded, though reluctantly. "Now, Hunter, I must apologize. I did not mean to pull you from London. I know you had a very important meeting tomorrow — today? Anyway, I'm fine, you can return whenever you—"

"Scarlett." He strode over and put a finger to her lips. "I didn't return today. I never even made it to London. I had turned around toward Wintervale and found you on the drive. You are incredible, that is for certain, to have had the strength to make it back. And I am so very glad you did."

"What do you mean you didn't make it to London?"

"I realized I had forgotten something more important than anything else in my life — you."

"Hunter," she said, not able to look into the ocean of his eyes, for then she would be lost and would forget all that she had to say. "I am sorry I was such a coward. I *will* return to London with you. I will be by your side, I promise. I was a fool, letting my own fears, my memories, my *parents*' life keep me from living my own. Forgive me, please?"

"No, love," Hunter said softly, sitting next to her now, his weight on the mattress causing her to roll toward him slightly. "I thought that I could bring you with me, to turn my life into our life, but I failed to realize that we must live together in what is best for both of us, not just for me. I love what I do in the House of Lords, I do, but I must admit that I become rather preoccupied with it, so much so that I often forgot to simply live. I will go once Session begins, and I would love to have you with me, but until then, here we will remain, enjoying life with one another. How does that sound?"

"But the work you are doing — it's important. Do you not need to be there?" she asked, her eyes round.

"I can speak with others through correspondence or with the odd visit to London. Thankfully Wintervale is not overly far," he said with a shrug, "But you — you I do need, Scarlett, and I have been a fool not to realize that until now."

She tried to throw herself in his arms but cringed when her chest tightened, and she sat back, gasping.

"Ah, yes," he said, wrinkling his nose. "The physician managed a visit yesterday, and he suspects you have bruised your chest, in addition to a sprained ankle. Both will heal quickly, mercifully, but you're going to have to be careful for a while. No riding. No activities that require any exertion."

"None?" she asked with a squeak.

He shook his head regretfully. "None, I'm afraid — for a few days at least."

"Ah, you had me worried there for a moment," she said with a wink, and he laughed, though he sobered when he saw the serious expression on her face.

"Are you in pain?" he asked, but she shook her head.

"No, it's simply that I have to tell you something, something that I should have quite some time ago. I love you, Hunter, with all of my heart," she said, having to clear her throat when she heard her voice begin to waver. "Since the day we were married, you have been nothing but kind and patient with me. I mistrusted you for no fault of your own and allowed fear to get the better of me. Which is silly, really, as I am fearful of nearly nothing else but losing my heart. Until I sat there in a snowbank, freezing down to my very bones, and I realized that what was even worse than my love going unrequited was not even giving it a chance."

He cupped her face in his hands, trailing his finger over the pattern of freckles on her nose and cheeks.

"I love you too, Scarlett," he said in nearly a whisper. "I've told you that many times before, but never did I realize how much until I saw you so numb with cold, looking as though blood could hardly be pumping through your veins any longer. I cannot lose you — I will not. You are my wife, Scarlett, and from now on, I am going to spend every day reminding you of the fact."

She began to smile, then, until tears began to flow down her face as her heart filled with all the love that was possible. Her smile stretched so wide that her cheeks ached, as he grinned back at her in return, reaching out to wipe away her tears. This was her husband, who loved her despite all that she had put him through.

"I was thinking," he said, picking up her hand once more, playing with her fingers. "If I need to return to London now and again, it is not far — only a few hours. I can go for a day or so at a time. Then I will return here, to you. When Session begins once more, however, then—"

"Then I will return with you," she said, holding up a hand when he made to argue. "I've decided this, and I will be fine with it. I have purpose — you've given me that with my charity work and foundation. And I am not returning alone. I am not returning to a man like my father, but to you,

Hunter Tannon. All you have to do is be yourself, and I shall be fine."

He leaned down then, and ever so gently brought his hands to either side of her head on the pillow, setting his lips against hers. He kissed her softly, a kiss full of promise of a life to come — together.

24

Twelfth Night ~ London

"This was a bad idea."

"Oh, don't be silly! I feel perfectly fine."

"Yes, but you should still be resting, not in London about to attend a ball."

"There is nowhere I would rather be, but on your arm."

Scarlett smiled at him so broadly that Hunter sighed, knowing she had won this argument, as she did most. When Scarlett turned that grin on him, he was lost, lost in her eyes and her loveliness. Not that he wouldn't tell her when she was wrong — for she certainly was, now and again. But today was a day for celebration.

"I shouldn't have let you come," he mumbled now as they arrived at Lord and Lady Totnes' home, where the Twelfth Night celebrations were taking place. "My meeting with Lord Falconer could have been over and done, and I could have been back at Wintervale with you. Instead—"

"Instead, we are taking part in these beautiful Twelfth

Night festivities," she finished. "Which I wanted to attend — with you."

He still wasn't completely convinced he should have allowed her to come, but she had been so persuasive that despite the doctor's orders, she had been out of bed and in his carriage seated next to him but a few days after her accident. She promised him she was feeling much better, and it was true that he could no longer see the pain in her eyes as he had even the day before.

Luckily, London was but a few hours from Wintervale, and so the carriage ride hadn't been long, and at the very least they were in plush conditions, with a warm stone on Scarlett's feet, a blanket over her legs, and Hunter's heated body at her back.

"I hope you didn't feel like you had to do this," he said, tilting his head down toward her now, "To prove to me that you could live in London."

"No," she shook her head. "I have to do this to prove to *myself* that this is not the London I remember, not the London of my parents. A new place, where we will make new memories."

"That we will," he nodded, winking wickedly at her. "I can assure you."

She swatted him good-naturedly but leaned back into him, and he tightened his arms around her as the carriage pulled to a stop.

"How do you find it so far, my Clara Courtlove?" She laughed and pushed away from him.

"Much better than anticipated," she responded, wiggling her eyebrows at him, her gaze trailing up and down his own dandy-ish costume. "Especially when one is accompanied by a man such as Samuel Strutt."

They were in their costumes for the evening. Having not

been in attendance at the previous night's festivities, their roles had been chosen for them, the cards sent to their London townhome. Hunter eyed Scarlett's particularly low bodice. He didn't much care for others to be looking upon it, but he reassured himself with the thought that only he would see what was underneath.

Hunter held out a hand to help Scarlett out of the carriage, and he didn't miss the deep breath she took before grasping it and walking down the steps and up the cobbled path and into the house. Facing the *ton* could be harrowing, to be sure — especially considering the fact that their marriage had been under a great deal of scrutiny during their three-month separation — but if anyone held the courage necessary to confront the rest of them, it was Scarlett, he thought, his already puffed chest sticking out even further than the design of his garish costume.

They had hardly taken a step in the door when their hosts nearly accosted them, and Hunter wanted to step in front of Scarlett and protect her, but it appeared she didn't need him as she gracefully greeted them. In fact, she soon charmed the crowd, though he didn't leave her side — most especially as she could hardly walk on her own, her ankle still as sore as it was. Mercifully, the physician's diagnosis of a sprain had proven correct, but it would be difficult for Scarlett to spend the night standing upon it. She was insistent, however, that she attend, and so he would do what he could to help her.

"Oxford! Don't tell me I finally have the chance to meet your beautiful wife?"

"Wimbledon!" Hunter's face stretched into a wide, genuine grin as a tall, handsome man strode over to the pair of them, reaching out an arm to greet her husband.

"I can see why he kept you hidden away," said Lord

Wimbledon with a wink. "He was afraid someone like me might attempt to steal you."

"Try as you might, Wimbledon," Hunter said good-naturedly, though he sent his friend a look of warning. "But you have no chance, I'm afraid."

Wimbledon winked at Scarlett, promised to sit next to her at dinner, and was on his way to flirt with the next women he found.

"Are you enjoying yourself, darling?" Hunter asked her as someone handed her a glass of champagne.

"I am, actually," she said, her eyes widening in surprise as she turned to look at him. "Certainly, there are those who choose to talk to us to determine the current status of our relationship, but there are some genuine souls here who seem to truly want to know me."

"How could they not?" he asked with a smile. "You are the most beautiful woman in the room."

"I doubt that," she said with a laugh.

"It's true," he said. "I know it is, even though I have hardly been able to look at another woman with you on my arm."

Her smile sent warmth shooting through his veins, right to his heart, and he vowed to spend the rest of his life ensuring that it remained on her face.

It seemed his promise would soon be put to the test, as he saw Scarlett's face fall into a frown, and he followed her gaze to the entrance of the room. Madeline. What were she and Jeremy doing here? He had thought they were to remain in the country until the spring.

The couple said not a word, but simply nodded to them as they walked by. *Please let this go well*, Hunter thought, as he stole another look at Scarlett. *Have them leave us alone.*

It was not to be, however, as after dinner Madeline walked directly their way.

"LADY OXFORD, MAY I HAVE A WORD?"

Why Madeline Lancaster wanted to speak with her, Scarlett had no idea, but she nodded, looking at Hunter to assure him all would be well. He helped her over to the settee in the corner of the drawing room, which was somewhat secluded from the remainder of the guests.

"I apologize for accosting you," Lady Raymond said once they were alone, though Hunter stood against a pillar a ways away watching them. "It is simply ... I was a beast, Lady Oxford," she said, hanging her head and completely taking Scarlett off guard.

"What?" Scarlett asked, wondering if she had heard her correctly.

"I said things to you that were not at all appropriate, no matter the state of your relationship. My own marriage ... well, it's not a particularly close one. And it's true I had always had something of a *tendre* for Hunter, and I didn't think the two of you were very ... attached. In fact, rumor was you hated him and forced him away from you and back to London."

Scarlett swallowed hard as the guilt rushed through her once more, for the woman was, in fact, correct regarding her previous actions.

"Anyway, it seems ... well, it seems I was entirely mistaken. One only has to watch the two of you for but a moment to see how wonderfully well you get on, how much you love one another. I hope for you the very best, and I promise to never come between you, nor say anything to suggest I will again."

"I—" Scarlett was so taken aback for a moment that she didn't know what to say. "Th-thank you Lady Raymond. I admit that I was rather insulted by your words at Christmas, though I suppose I was as upset as much by my own behavior that would lead you to your assumptions as I was angry at you for saying such a thing. As we are neighbors, however, and each close with Lavinia, I would suggest we put it behind us."

"Oh, I'm so glad," said Lady Raymond, taking her hands. "And now, sadly, this may be our last words for the night as my character is that of Maud Mute."

Her expression was so distressed that Scarlett nearly laughed, but she choked it back as Lady Raymond didn't seem to find the humor in it.

"Very well, Lady Raymond," she said. "We will be returning to the country very soon, so I am sure we will see you there."

"Both of you?" she asked, her eyes raised.

"Both of us," Scarlett confirmed with a smile, which Lady Raymond simply returned knowingly and walked away.

It wasn't long after the Twelfth Night cake had been served and the revelries began in earnest that Hunter leaned down to murmur in Scarlett's ear, a thrill coursing through her when she felt his breath tickle her neck.

"Are you feeling well?" he asked, and she looked at him with surprise, nodding. "Of course. I would tell you if I wasn't."

"I think..." he cleared his throat, "that perhaps you need a moment away from the crowd, to relax if you will."

"No, I don't— oh!" she finally noticed the gleam in his

eyes, filled with meaning as he looked suggestively down at her, and her pulse began to pound. "I suppose I am feeling a tad unwell, my lord, and I believe I must take a moment to compose myself," she said, slightly louder, grinning up at him wickedly. He rolled his eyes, apparently not entirely impressed by her acting skills, but he took her arm in his once more and led her out of the room. Scarlett felt like running through the long corridor, but with her limp, their progress was much slower. Hunter looked within a few doorways before finally finding one that was to his liking.

"Why this room?" she asked as he led her into the drawing room, where the fire in the hearth warmly greeted them.

"It has a lock," he said, raising an eyebrow. "And it's empty."

"You mean the other rooms..."

"It's a night of celebration," he said with a shrug and a grin, and Scarlett was momentarily shocked. "Though," he continued. "We may be the only married couple to find ourselves ensconced together in one of the Totnes' drawing rooms."

"I wouldn't want it any other way," she said, stepping closer to him, her fingers fisting in his shirt. That was all he seemed to need to swoop down on her, his lips descending on hers as though he had been starved of her for days — which, she supposed he was, as they hadn't made love since her fall.

Their hands were everywhere as they explored one another as though they were strangers, a rush descending upon them in a new setting, in costumes, in a place where someone could walk in on them at any moment. And yet, despite all of the differences from their previous times together, what mattered most — Hunter, her husband —

remained constant. Scarlett could sense how carefully he handled her, the lightness of his hands causing all of her nerves to jump on edge, bumps to rise on her skin. She wasn't sure if it was the roaring fire or Hunter's ministrations, but she felt flushed all over, from her head to her toes. Her hair, arranged according to her character, already cascaded around her shoulders, and Hunter took full advantage of that fact, weaving his fingers into it, digging them into her scalp as he took her lips in his, tasting, teasing, promising more to come.

"Hunter," she gasped.

He broke away from her to murmur, "That is Samuel Strutt to you, my love," causing her to laugh, and a thrill coursed through her at the thought that this man would be teasing her for the rest of her life.

It was worth it, to be with him, by his side at all times. It was worth it to leave her home for a time, and, more than she could have ever thought possible, it was worth it to risk her heart. For if one didn't give it at all, there really was nothing to lose, and that was the greatest tragedy of all.

Could a man possibly be any luckier?

The frigid woman he had thought he married those months ago had entirely disappeared, melted away by the fire that was truly Scarlett. She kissed him now with more passion than he would have thought possible for any woman to hold within her, and the restraint of holding himself back, to keep from aggravating her injuries, was killing him.

Hunter slowed down for a moment, bringing his hands to Scarlett's back, grateful to find that this costume dress was laced down the back. With one swift motion, he had the ties undone, and the gown slipped easily from her shoulders, where it had been just hanging on. The sleeves dipped down the satiny skin of her arms, the round tops of her breasts peeking out from above her chemise.

He groaned as he brushed his fingers against their cushiony tops, wanting more — needing more. As much as he yearned to completely undress her, in the recesses of his mind he knew how much difficulty it would cause if his wife had to hurriedly redress. Instead, he picked up Scarlett as gently as he could and laid her on the chesterfield which bracketed the fireplace. He slid his hands up her legs, the garters of her stockings causing him a thrill as he navigated his way through the folds of her gown.

"What are you doing?" she breathed.

"Do not worry so much about that," he murmured. "Simply enjoy."

For once, she listened to him, as he found her small nub of pleasure and began to stroke it, first with his fingers, and then with his mouth. He made love to her, taking great pleasure in her groans and cries of delight, until she was kicking at him, calling his name.

"Hunter, I can't … I can't take it any longer. I want to feel you — please?"

He could certainly comply with that request.

"Well," he said, quickly unfastening the fall of his trousers, sending them to the floor as he leaned over her, "since you asked so nicely."

And in nearly one motion he sheathed himself within her, groaning at the feel of her, tight and wet. He gripped her firm bottom in both hands, moving in and out of her slowly, not wanting to jostle her, to cause pain to her ribs.

"Scarlett," he groaned, wanting nothing more than to

lose himself in her, but knowing he had to be as tender as possible.

"Faster," she said, urging him on, and when he kept himself in control, she began to move against him, impatient that he wouldn't comply.

"Stop, you'll hurt yourself," he said, bringing his hands to her hips, which seemed so small under his long fingers, but he began to do as she asked, thrusting quicker, in and out. He brought his thumb back to her most sensitive place, and the moment he touched her she cried out his name, convulsing around him, sending him over the edge himself, as he poured himself into her with a bellow.

He collapsed over her, keeping his weight on his elbows, which framed her head.

"My God, Scarlett," he said, trying to bring his breathing back under control. "You never cease to amaze me."

"Me?" she said with a startled laugh. "You did all of the work!"

"Yes," he said with a half grin of self-satisfaction. "I suppose I did."

He sat up, bringing her with him, and despite her protestations that she could dress, he helped her to fasten and straighten her gown, to rearrange her hair.

"How do I look?" she asked.

"Stunning," he said sincerely, and while she laughed at him, he could see the gratitude in her eyes.

"Well, my love," he asked. "How has London met with your expectations so far?"

"It has been altogether lovely," she said. "Better than anything I could have ever imagined."

"And your memories now?"

"Of the most wonderful Twelfth Night I could have asked for, and a husband I didn't know was waiting for me."

At the earnest look in her eyes, in the midst of her imperfect yet, at the same time, so utterly perfect face, Hunter dropped his forehead to hers. "I shall always be faithful to you. Forever and always," he promised.

"And I to you. I love you, Hunter Tannon."

"And I you, Scarlett Tannon."

EPILOGUE

December 24, 1814

"Spicer?" Scarlett called. "Would you mind fetching the library stairs?"

"Not at all, my lady," said her husband's valet with a quick grin. Scarlett didn't miss the wink he sent in the direction of her maid, who was now his wife. How wonderfully it had turned out for them, she thought wistfully.

Once Spicer had returned to Oak Hall, Scarlett took the mistletoe ball in hand, ready to hang it in the same place as last year.

"Do you suppose, Marion, it's silly to want to decorate as similar to what we did previously?" she asked her maid.

"Not at all, my lady," Marion replied. "Tradition is important."

"You are right," said Scarlett with a nod. "And we are beginning new traditions." She was two steps up when Hunter came charging into the room.

"What do you think you are doing?" he burst out, and

for a moment, Scarlett stopped in shock. Was he really protesting the Christmas decorations once again this year?

"Hanging the mistletoe," she said, but before she even knew what was happening, he had picked her up and placed her on the floor, plucking the bough from her hand.

"Please do not continually try to kill yourself decorating this house," he said, shaking his head, and Scarlett chuckled as he leaned up to hang the bough on the hook in the doorframe. "Now," he continued, stepping off the ladder. "We must ensure this mistletoe has been hung correctly."

"Oh?" she said, raising an eyebrow. "And how do you propose to do that?"

"If you'll take a step this way," he took her arm and led her two paces forward. "We shall now see."

Scarlett looked up, saw the bough overhead, and smiled at Hunter, but soon her lips were otherwise occupied, by his moving over hers. If it wasn't for the fact they were surrounded by servants, she didn't know where the kiss might lead, but soon Hunter broke away, with a promise of "tonight," in her ear as he slipped away. He didn't go far, however, simply to the corner, where greenery was piled, ready to adorn the household.

"Well," he said, "we better get to work if we'd like to complete the entire house by this evening."

Scarlett grinned. It seemed the man who had previously despaired of Christmas had had a change of heart.

"What special gift would you like for Christmas this year?"

"Do not tell me you haven't already prepared it?" she asked, and he grinned at her, teasing.

"I suppose I would simply like to know how close I am to what you truly want," he said, and she smiled at him. "You have already given me all I could ask for," she said. "The opportunity and the freedom to help others when I please. I appreciate what you have done more than you know."

"You are the one with unsurpassed talent and generosity," he said, and Scarlett's cheeks warmed as she turned away from his unwanted yet admirable praise.

The next hour flew by so fast that Scarlett was shocked when one of the maids entered the room, calling to her. "My lady? You asked me to inform you when Holly awoke."

Scarlett practically ran from the room, up to the nursery, with Hunter following close behind her. Would she ever tire of this, of holding her daughter in her arms? She took the baby from the nursemaid and held her close, sinking into the rocking chair, inhaling the sweet fresh scent of her child.

Holly had been born three months before, and Hunter called her his Christmas gift, as that was when their love began, resulting in their child. Scarlett looked at him now, as he crouched next to her chair, and they shared a smile of contentment over all the joys they shared together.

Scarlett closed her eyes for a moment as she thought of how painful her life could have been if she had kept Hunter frozen away from her forever. Instead, they now shared a life of joy, of warmth, and of love. So unlike her parents' own unhappy marriage, although Scarlett's mother had been overcome with happiness at Holly's birth. That reminded her...

"Oh, Hunter?" she said, hating to break this moment, but needing to tell him before she forgot. "My, uh, parents may come to visit, but just for a day or so. My mother desperately wanted to come spend time with Holly, and my father insisted as well..."

She trailed off at his look of horror. "My parents are coming as well," he said with a bit of a strangled noise, and despite her share of his dismay, she had to laugh at the expression on his face.

"Oh dear," she said, biting her lip. "This could make for an interesting Christmas."

"It could indeed," he said, nodding his head slowly. "But this year, my love, there is nothing, and no one, that can detract from our love, nor our trust in one another."

"I agree," she said, smiling at him and holding Holly close. "Whatever comes our way — jealous ladies, snow-storms, or even meddling parents — we will face them together."

"So we shall," he said, leaning in to place a quick kiss on her lips, before kissing Holly's forehead.

"Happy Christmas, my love."

"Happy Christmas."

THE DUKE SHE WISHED FOR

HAPPILY EVER AFTER BOOK 1

PREVIEW
Go back to the beginning and read the story of Tabitha and
Nicholas...

CHAPTER 1

The creak of the shop's front door opening floated through the heavy curtains that separated Tabitha's workshop from the sales floor. She tensed over the silk ribbon she was attempting to fashion into a flower shape and waited for the sound of her stepsister Frances to greet whoever had just walked into the Blackmore Milliner shop.

She paused, waiting a little bit longer before pushing out a frustrated breath and standing. These velvet ribbon flowers she had learned to fashion were part of the reason Blackmore hats sat atop some of the finest female heads in polite society — she had a knack for creating new ways to adorn the same old bonnet or beaver hat styles so that a woman of a certain class stood out among her peers.

This ability was both a blessing and a curse, it turned out. Her creativity meant Tabitha brought customers through the front door, to the shop she and her father had built after her mother died when she was seven years old. It had brought Tabitha and her father, the baronet Elias Blackmore, closer together in their time of immeasurable grief, and the shop had flourished.

The relationship between father and daughter remained strong, and when she was twelve years of age, he approached her and told her he wanted to marry a baroness from the North Country. The baroness had a daughter about her own age, he'd added. Tabitha had been happy for her father and excited at the prospect of having a sister. She had welcomed her new family with an open heart and open arms.

What a silly little fool she'd been, Tabitha thought with derisive snort as she pushed herself to her feet and through the brocade curtains to greet the newcomer. Lord only knew where Frances had gone off to. Likely shopping with her mother, Ellora.

Upon the untimely death of Sir Elias Blackmore three years after the marriage, Tabitha had been utterly devastated. Lady Blackmore, however, hadn't wasted much time in putting Tabitha in her place. No longer the family's most cherished daughter, Tabitha had been shoved into the workroom and largely ignored, but for her skills as a milliner — they kept just enough of her stepmother's attention on her.

The more she stood up to Ellora, the more her stepmother threatened to throw her out on the street. Knowing it was within Ellora's nature to follow through on her threat, Tabitha did her best to ignore and avoid her stepmother, focusing instead on her work and her ambitions.

It was better, Tabitha supposed, than staying in their townhome all day long worrying about social calls that never came or invitations that would never arrive. The family name had suffered greatly under Lady Blackmore and Miss Frances Denner, her daughter from a previous marriage.

In truth, Tabitha was little more than a servant with no money to speak of, no family to lean on, and no real prospects other than her creations on which to pin her hopes of ever escaping the lot she'd been given after her father died.

In the showroom, Tabitha scanned the floor in search of the new arrival. It took a moment, but her eyes finally landed on a small, older man in a fine suit. He had a slip of paper in his hand, and he approached Tabitha with the air of someone who didn't waste time.

"Good afternoon, Miss," the man began with perfect, practiced speech. "My name is Mr. McEwan. I serve as the steward in the house of Her Grace the Duchess of Stowe. I have a receipt for a series of hats I believe she had ordered, and she is requesting that they be delivered tomorrow afternoon."

Tabitha felt her stomach sink. If this was the order she was thinking of, the one currently on her worktable, there was no way under the stars that the three hats would be ready by tomorrow. She was only one flower (out of seven) into the first bonnet, and it was a slow process to convince the requested velvet ribbon to behave.

"I am sorry, sir," she began, trying to get his eyes off the wilder ostrich-plumed hats next to her and back on her. "That is almost four days before we agreed upon. I'm certain there is no feasible way the work can be done, and done well, by tomorrow."

That got the older man's attention. He huffed, turned a bit pink around the cheeks, and sputtered.

"There is simply no choice, my dear," he said abruptly but not unkindly. "His Grace is arriving home from his trip to France early and therefore the parties his mother has planned for him will be adjusted accordingly. And so, her wardrobe *must* be ready — she said so herself. She is willing to pay handsomely for your ability to expedite the process."

Tabitha drew in a breath at that and considered. She was having such a difficult time scrimping a small savings together to buy herself a seat at the Paris School of Millinery that this "bonus" money might perhaps get her there that much quicker. Assuming, of course, that Ellora didn't catch wind of the extra earnings. She was quick to snatch up all but the barest pennies.

Tabitha closed her eyes for a moment and drew a steadying breath. If she worked through the night and her needle and thread held true, there was a *slight* chance that she could finish in time. She said so to Mr. McEwan, who beamed brightly at her.

"I knew it," he said with a laugh. "I have faith you Miss — er, I apologize, I did not hear your name?"

Tabitha sighed.

"Tabitha Blackmore," she said, noticing how quickly he'd changed the subject on her. "I did not exactly say that I would be able to—"

She was cut off again by Mr. McEwan, who gave her a slight bow and provided directions to the home of the Dowager Duchess of Stowe on the other side of the city.

"I shall see you tomorrow, then, my dear," he said with a quick grin. "Be sure to pack a bag to stay at least one evening, maybe two. I am certain Her Grace's attendants will need proper coaching on how best to pair the hats. You will be paid, of course!"

With that the short man with wisps of white hair on his head that stood up like smoke was gone, disappearing into the streets of Cheapside.

Tabitha leaned back against the counter behind her and blew out a breath, a little overwhelmed at the entire encounter.

On the one hand, she had found a way to increase her

savings and take a step closer to the education her father had wanted for her. On the other, getting through the night in one piece was not guaranteed. She would have to return to the shop after dinner and do so without rousing Lady Blackmore's suspicions, which would not be easy.

Tabitha kicked at a crushed crepe ribbon flower that hadn't been tossed out properly. Another evening down the back drainpipe it was, then.

"Time away from the witch, I suppose," she muttered as she returned to her worktable, a new fire of inspiration lit beneath her.

Dinner was more complicated than usual, thanks to the fact that Ellora, Tabitha's stepmother, was having one of her *moods*. They could be brought on by anything — the weather (too foul or too pleasant), the noisy street they lived on, memories of her life when she was the daughter of an earl and had endless opportunities for money and titles, or even an egg that had too much salt.

Today's mood, however, had more to do with the fact that her daughter Frances had been recently snubbed. Officially, Ellora was considered a member of the *ton* and her daughter's first season the previous year had nearly cost them the roof over their heads. However, Frances was an ill-tempered, sharp-tongued girl who did little to ensure repeat invitations to dances and parties.

"A true-and-true witch," their housekeeper, Alice, called her. Alice was the only servant left on staff besides Katie, the lady's maid Ellora and Frances shared, so it was up to both Alice and Tabitha to make sure that meals were made and rooms were kept clean. Being an indentured servant in her own home was trying enough, but much worse was having to tidy the room that once held every memento of her father's. It was now completely devoid of every memory of him.

It was as though Baronet Elias Blackmore had never existed. No portraits. No personal belongings. Nothing but the small locket he'd given Tabitha when she was nine years old, which she still wore around her neck.

This evening's dinner was a morose affair, and Tabitha sat silently while Ellora ranted and raved about the social snub of her angel, Frances.

Tabitha looked across the table at her stepsister. Frances was very pretty, she'd give her that much. But her mouth was drawn thin and her blue eyes were more steely than pleasant. Frances had brown hair that one could call more dishwater in color than brunette. However, Ellora spent high sums of money on beauty products and bits and bobs for Katie to fashion Frances' hair into something resembling high fashion each day.

Frances was pouting into her soup while her mother railed beside her. When she glanced up and caught Tabitha looking at her, she scowled.

Tabitha quickly looked away, but Frances jumped on the opportunity to take the attention off her.

"I saw a servant go into the shop this afternoon when I was returning from tea with Adela," Frances said to her mother, her flinty eyes on Tabitha, who inwardly groaned.

So much for secrecy.

Ellora paused in her ranting and raised an eyebrow at her.

"Who was it?"

The words were clipped, and her nose was high in the air while she peered along it at Tabitha.

"A servant for the Dowager Duchess of Stowe," Tabitha replied. "He came to inquire about an order the Duchess sent over a week ago."

It wasn't exactly a lie and it helped her corroborate her story because Ellora had already received the money sent over for the original order.

"And was the order ready?"

Tabitha swallowed hard. She wasn't in the clear yet.

"Almost," she said and lowered her eyes to take a sip of the soup as she inwardly seethed.

"Unacceptable," her stepmother ground out between her teeth. "You lazy, no-good hanger-on. It is no wonder your father's ridiculous hat shop is dying off. He had the laziest cow this side of the river working behind the curtains."

She banged a fist on the table, making Frances jump.

"You get up from this table and you finish that order right this instant." Ellora pointed a long bony finger in the direction of the door, ending Tabitha's dinner before she had progressed past the soup. Tabitha's stomach rumbled in protest, and her fists clenched beneath the table as she longed to tell Ellora what she really thought, but Tabitha knew this was a gift. She would nab a roll from Alice later.

"I am going to stop by in the morning to check your ledger and work progress to make certain you are being completely honest with me," Ellora announced. "And woe be to you if I find that you have been neglecting your work and you have a backlog of orders."

In reality, Tabitha was of legal age and the threats should be harmless. But she was also lacking any real money, any job prospects, and had no titles her father could have passed down to her. Running her father's milliner shop was the closest thing she would have to freedom for the near future, and it would be much better for her if she allowed Ellora the illusion of control for the time being, since the dreadful woman had inherited the shop upon her father's death.

Ellora's threat put Tabitha in a bind. She was due at the Duchess' estate first thing in the morning. As it stood, she'd have to have those pieces done, as well as the other orders on her workbench before then. She closed her eyes and blew out a heavy breath.

It was going to be a very long night.

The Duke She Wished For is now available for purchase on Amazon, and is free to read through Kindle Unlimited.

QUEST OF HONOR

SEARCHING HEARTS BOOK 1

PREVIEW
Begin the stories of the Harrington family with Thomas and
Eleanor...

PROLOGUE

Marie looked around the table at her five children, her gaze coming to rest on Thomas. Normally she was most concerned about Daniel, her eldest and the next in line to become Duke, but there was something about Thomas tonight that seemed off to her.

Typically the most free-spirited of her children, this evening he wore a serious look, and had taken on the brooding silence that overcame him whenever he felt stifled or frustrated.

The remainder of her children, from Daniel at 24 down to her 16-year-old daughter Polly, were chattering away as they were normally wont to do, no matter how she tried to instil in them the proper etiquette of the dinner hour. Her husband, Lionel, Duke of Ware, sat in his usual place at the head of the table, intent on his food as he listened to the stories of his brood.

"Thomas," Marie said, and he raised his dark head. "Is everything quite well, darling?"

"Yes, Mother," he replied mechanically.

"Are you quite sure?"

"Well actually," he said, looking hesitantly at her and then his father. "I do have somewhat of an announcement."

Marie raised her eyebrows as the chatter around the table hushed, for Thomas' siblings could see the nervousness that accompanied his statement.

"I am going to be joining the Navy," he said, puffing his chest out, trying to look more assured than he felt.

"The Navy!" his mother exclaimed incredulously. "You cannot be serious. Is this some sort of joke?"

"Not at all, Mother," he responded, his blue eyes taking on an icy resolve. "The Navy is a noble profession. What else am I to do with my life?"

"You are the second son of a Duke! What if the title of Duke should need to pass onto you and you are injured or dead somewhere at sea?"

"I shall not spend my life sitting here waiting for Father and Daniel to die, Mother," he responded, his voice becoming slightly more heated, although he would never raise it at his mother. "They are both quite healthy and, I'm sure, have long lives to live. I want to see the world! What better way than on the sea?"

"Lionel!" Marie said to her husband with fervour. "Have you nothing to say?"

Lionel finished chewing his potatoes, his expression unwavering.

"Well, son," he said. "I would say your intentions are admirable. You do know what you are getting yourself into?"

"I do."

"Well, then, boy, I'd best talk to my friend the Admiral tomorrow. The son of the Duke of Ware must find a reasonable berth and vessel upon which to serve."

Thomas' face lit up, and he caught the gaze of his sister

Violet, who smiled at him encouragingly. He grinned at her, then turned back to his father.

"Thank you, Father," he said. "I would appreciate it."

"This is quite ridiculous," his mother said, her head swivelling from Thomas to Lionel and back to Thomas once more. "Thomas is 22 years old! He and Daniel should be finding wives, settling down, raising children. Instead, Daniel is out doing Heaven knows what and Thomas will be at sea miles away from Britain! How is it that I have three children of marriageable age, none of which have any interest in actually being married?"

Benjamin and Polly smirked, happy to have the attention off of them and onto their three elder siblings.

"In due time, Mother," said Violet, somewhat mollifying her. "In due time. In the meantime, let us drink to Thomas and the world that awaits him."

"To Thomas!" They all joined in, with the exception of Marie, and Thomas grinned, excited about what the future would hold for him.

1

___

Eleanor Adams sat primly on the straight backed chair as her father stomped around, muttering something under his breath. She waited patiently for his judgement to fall, knowing that he would not be able to bring himself to punish her too severely. After all, she was his only child and he had never been able to be too strict with her. In fact, this was the only life Eleanor had ever known. Just her and her father, facing the world and all its tribulations.

"You cannot simply do as you please, Eleanor!" her father spluttered, his face now a beetroot red. "What if we had not seen you?"

Eleanor stifled a sigh of frustration. "Papa, you know me better than that. I simply *had* to investigate whatever it was down there." A small smile crept across her face. "And, if I had not, then we would currently not have these three small trunks in our possession." She indicated the three, still

235

damp, trunks that sat beside her father's desk, glancing at them before returning her gaze to her father.

To her very great relief, he sighed and sat down heavily, although he continued to shake his head at her. Eleanor hid her smile. She was triumphant.

"We have not opened them yet, Eleanor," her father said, a little gruffly. "You could have risked your life for nothing."

In response, Eleanor tossed her head, aware of the spots of moisture that shook off her long flaxen locks. "I am one of the best swimmers among the crew, Papa, you know that."

"But still," he retorted. "You cannot just dive off the ship without alerting someone to what you have found! Had you done so, I could have dropped the anchor and gone to see what was there."

Eleanor bit her lip, aware that her father was being more than reasonable. Had any one of his crew done what she had, they would have been severely punished. It was only because she was the captain's daughter that she had done such a thing. Her cheeks warmed. "I was trying to prove myself, Papa," she explained, more quietly. "As the only woman on board, I have to take extra steps to show my worth."

His face softened. "Eleanor, you already have my respect and the respect of the crew. For over twenty years you have traveled the seas with us and you have no need to prove yourself. Doing such a thing is both dangerous and shows a lack of regard for me – not only as your father but also as your captain." His lined face grew more serious, as his bushy eyebrows clung together. "You know that I will need to punish you for what you did, Eleanor. As much as it pains me to do this, you are to be confined to your quarters for two days."

"Two days?" Eleanor gasped, staring at her father. "But I will miss the exploration!"

Her father nodded gravely. "I have to show the crew that I am not afraid to punish you, even though you are my daughter." A hint of a smile pulled up the corner of his lips. "Just be glad it is not the cat o'nine tails, Eleanor."

Eleanor sagged against the chair, her ladylike position gone in a moment. Reflecting on her father's decision, she had to admit that it was fair, lenient even. She hated that her impulsive nature had, once again, brought severe consequences. If only she had not dived into the water to see what it was that glistened below! If she had only told her father, then he would have dropped the anchor and sent someone down – although Eleanor doubted that he would have chosen her. Even though she could swim like a fish, her father always kept her in his sights whenever he could.

"I am sorry you will miss the exploration of the Blackmoor Caves," her father continued, gently. "But Eleanor, you must know that you cannot simply do what you please on this ship."

"I do know, Papa," Eleanor replied, dully, ashamed that her the whole ordeal caused her to feel like a child when she would prefer to be treated as the sailor she was. She could only hope the treasure would yield results that would make all forget about the find and focus on the outcome. "I'm sorry."

Her father placed a gentle hand on her shoulder, getting to his feet. "Like you say, however, we have retrieved three trunks."

Hope sparked in Eleanor's chest. "You mean, I can open them?"

He chuckled. "I think so. After all, you were the one who spotted the locks gleaming under the ocean's waves."

Eleanor rose, her booted feet clattering across the wooden floor of the cabin as she made her way towards the trunks. She would have to change into dry clothing, but that could wait. "It is only because we are in such shallow waters," she said, bending down to examine the trunks. "Had the water been any deeper, then I doubt we would have found them."

"Here." Her father handed her a large mallet, and, using all her strength, Eleanor hit the lock.

It broke easily, evidently having been underwater for some time. With bated breath, Eleanor pushed the top of the trunk back. A wide grin spread across her face as she took in the bounty.

"There is some gold here," she cried, pulling out a gold coin and handing it to her father. "Not much, but enough."

Chuckling, her father picked up the mallet and broke the other two locks, finding more gold and some silver in the other two trunks. He crowed with delight as he grasped great handfuls of coins, letting them trickle back down into the trunk. Despite her impending punishment, Eleanor could not help but smile too, delighted that they would have more than enough to pay the crew for the next quarter.

"Everyone shall have a bonus!" her father declared, getting to his feet and throwing open the door to his cabin. "Morgan!"

The first mate came stumbling in, as though he'd been waiting for the captain to call his name. "Aye, Captain Adams?"

Eleanor grinned as her father slapped Morgan on the back, before gesturing towards the treasure.

"Here," he said. "Sort this out. Crew's pay and a bonus for everyone. Leave the remaining treasure in the first trunk."

Morgan returned Eleanor's smile, and got to the task at once, jubilant over some of the wonders he was finding. It would take him an age to sort out the treasure into piles of equal worth, but Eleanor knew it was a job the first mate thoroughly enjoyed.

Wiping down her breeches, Eleanor got to her feet and smiled at her father, wondering if he might forget her punishment.

Unfortunately, he had not.

"Right, Eleanor, to your cabin. Your meals will be sent down."

A sigh left her lips as she trudged past him, sniffing inelegantly. Behind her, she heard her father chuckle.

"Two days will be over before you know it, my dear," he said, following her out. "And if we find anything at the caves, you may join in the salvaging."

That was a slight relief, making her shoulders rise from their slumped position. "Thank you, Papa," she mumbled, as the fresh air hit her lungs. Taking in another few breaths, Eleanor took in the smell of the sea, the wind whipping at her hair....before she realized that the entire crew was watching her.

Taking a breath, she lifted her chin. "I should not have dived off the boat without alerting someone to what I had found," she said, loudly. "I did you all wrong by acting so impulsively and showed disrespect to our captain. I will not do such a thing again." She caught the look of sympathy in some of the crew's eyes, although they appeared to be relieved that she was receiving some kind of punishment. Without another word, Eleanor turned on her heel and walked down the short staircase to her cabin below.

Being the only woman meant she had one of only two tiny cabins below deck – Morgan, the first mate, held the other. Pulling open the door, she looked glumly into her gloomy room, hating that she would be stuck inside for two days.

"Thank you for your apology, Eleanor," her father said, holding the door as she walked inside. "The crew respects you, as they do me. They will hold you in greater esteem because you have confessed your wrongs."

Eleanor tried to smile, sitting down heavily on the wooden bed. "Thank you, Papa. I believe the treasure I found for them may also have increased their sense of 'esteem' in me."

He grinned at her. "You're a pirate's daughter, Eleanor. Some might think that means we have no standards, no way of keeping control, but you know how precarious the sea – and the crew – can be. They are loyal to me, and I want them to be loyal to you too. One day, this boat might be yours." With a quick smile, he closed the door and left her to her thoughts.

Eleanor stared at the door, her father's words echoing around her mind. One day, she might have control of the ship? Be the captain? Could such a thing truly happen?

Eleanor knew that in the Navy, there would be no thought of having a female captain, but they were far removed from the Navy! Pirates did things differently and, if her father thought the crew would respect her as captain, then she would gladly step into the role, though she hoped it would be some time before her father gave it up and retired from the seas.

To be a pirate captain! The thought made her smile, despite her current situation. To roam the seas with her crew, searching for bounty and, in their case, helping those less fortunate. She could not think of a better life.

QUEST OF HONOR is now available for purchase on Amazon and to read free in Kindle Unlimited!

MORE FROM ELLIE ST. CLAIR

Sign-up for the email list and get a free Regency Romance
"Unmasking a Duke" sent straight to your inbox.
You will also receive links to updates, launch information,
promos, limited time sales, and the newest recommended
reads. An opportunity to join my advance reader team may
also be available.

SIGN-UP HERE:

www.prairielilypress.com/ellies-newsletter/

ABOUT THE AUTHOR

Ellie has always loved reading, writing, and history. For many years she has written short stories, non-fiction, and has worked on her true love and passion -- romance novels.

In every era there is the chance for romance, and Ellie enjoys exploring many different time periods, cultures, and geographic locations. No matter when or where, love can always prevail. She has a particular soft spot for the bad boys of history, and loves a strong heroine in her stories.

The lake is Ellie's happy place, and when she's not writing, she is spending time with her son, her Husky/Border Collie cross, and her own dashing duke. She loves reading — of course — as well as running, biking, and summers at the lake.

She also loves corresponding with readers, so be sure to contact her!

www.prairielilypress.com/ellie-st-clair
ellie@prairielilypress.com

facebook.com/elliestclairauthor

twitter.com/ellie_stclair

instagram.com/elliestclairauthor

amazon.com/author/elliestclair

goodreads.com/elliestclair

bookbub.com/authors/elliest.clair

pinterest.com/elliestclair

ALSO BY ELLIE ST. CLAIR

Standalone

Unmasking a Duke

Christmastide with His Countess

Seduced Under the Mistletoe Multi-Author Box Set

(featuring The Duke of Christmas)

Happily Ever After

The Duke She Wished For

Someday Her Duke Will Come

Once Upon a Duke's Dream

He's a Duke, But I Love Him

Loved by the Viscount

Because the Earl Loved Me

Searching Hearts

Quest of Honor

Clue of Affection

Hearts of Trust

Hope of Romance

Promise of Redemption

Made in the USA
Middletown, DE
12 February 2019